"Run for your called. *"The dam has broken!"*

His shout snapped Betsy and Warren out of their shock and into action. "Take this," Betsy said, tossing the life ring to the man.

"Let's get out of here," Warren said. He reached for the On button of the Instant Commuter.

"We have to try to save Anna. We should have about five minutes before the water gets up here."

Pursued by the rapidly rising water, they dashed back to the Keeton home and pounded on the door.

This time Mrs. Keeton opened the door. Water covered the threshold and crept across the wooden floor. When Mrs. Keeton saw who it was, she started to shut the door.

Betsy cried out, "The dam has burst! You have three minutes to save your child!"

The water swirled around them—first up to their ankles, then up to their knees—

Their time was running out . . .

Books by Peg Kehret

Available from MINSTREL Books

THE FLOOD DISASTER

PEG KEHRET

A MINSTREL® BOOK

Published by POCKET BOOKS
New York   London   Toronto   Sydney   Tokyo   Singapore

A Minstrel Book published by
POCKET BOOKS, a division of Simon & Schuster Inc.
1230 Avenue of the Americas, New York, NY 10020

Copyright © 1999 by Peg Kehret

Originally published in hardcover in 1999 by Minstrel Books

All rights reserved, including the right to reproduce
this book or portions thereof in any form whatsoever.
For information address Pocket Books, 1230 Avenue
of the Americas, New York, NY 10020

ISBN: 1416991093
ISBN: 978-1-4169-9109-0

First Minstrel Books paperback printing October 1999

10 9 8 7 6 5 4 3 2 1

A MINSTREL BOOK and colophon are registered trademarks of
Simon & Schuster Inc.

Front cover illustration by Bill Schmidt

Printed in the U.S.A.

*For Ilise Levine,
with thanks for her good advice,
constant support, and the memorable
hotel tantrum*

ACKNOWLEDGMENTS

I want to acknowledge David McCullough, author of *The Johnstown Flood*, which was originally published in 1968 and is now available as a Touchstone Book from Simon & Schuster. Mr. McCullough's thorough research made my task easier.

I also thank Lee and Norm Paasch for lending me their copy of *History of the Great Flood*, a book of recollections of the people who lived through this event plus news articles that were printed at the time. This was published by J. S. Ogilvie in 1889. Although the book contains inaccuracies, the first-hand descriptions gave me insight into the daily lives of the people of Johnstown, their speech patterns, and their philosophies, as well as gruesome details of the tragedy.

CHAPTER

1

"Fireflies aren't really flies," said Betsy Tyler, "and glowworms aren't really worms."

She and Warren Spalding were in their class on natural disasters, waiting while Mr. Munson handed out the new assignments.

"They aren't?" Warren said. He wondered why writing a report on a natural disaster would make Betsy's mind skip to fireflies and glowworms, but he was used to her quirky memory. Betsy often dropped odd facts into a conversation for no apparent reason.

"Glowworms and fireflies are related, and they are both actually beetles. The males have wings and fly around at night, especially in warm weather. They sparkle like tiny stars, and they're called fireflies, or lightning bugs. The females look like worms; they produce a steady greenish-blue light, and they're known as glowworms. In some species even the eggs glow!"

"No kidding," said Warren. Although Betsy's peculiar facts always surprised him, he had to admit that they were interesting. With Betsy for a classroom partner Warren never got bored.

Mr. Munson handed Warren the new assignment.

Warren Spalding/Betsy Tyler
The Johnstown Flood, May 31, 1889.

"Do you know anything about the Johnstown flood?" Warren asked Betsy.

"No. But we'll learn, just like we learned about the eruption of Mount Saint Helens, and the Armistice Day blizzard."

Scary memories of thick volcanic ash on Mount Saint Helens and blinding snow in

2

The Flood Disaster

Minnesota crowded into the corners of Warren's mind. When Warren moved in with his grandmother while his mother finished her college degree, he had found the Instant Commuter, a machine invented by his late grandfather. Twice Betsy and Warren had used the device to travel through space and time. They had gone back to the scenes of their first two class assignments and had experienced the disasters in person.

Both trips had ended in catastrophe. The two kids barely escaped the eruption of the volcano and were nearly trapped forever in the blizzard.

Mr. Munson finished handing out the assignments, then knocked on his desk to get the attention of the class. "These reports are to be twenty-five pages long," he said, "and I want you to include a visual display, such as some artwork, charts, or photographs."

Instantly the room sounded as if every student had a terrible stomachache. Moans and groans mixed with whines and complaints.

"The first two reports were only twenty

pages long," said Warren's friend Skipper. "Why does this one have to be twenty-five?"

"You're more experienced now," Mr. Munson said. "You won't keep improving unless you're challenged."

"I was plenty challenged," Skipper said, "by twenty pages."

"Twenty-five," said Mr. Munson. "They are due three weeks from today, and the sooner you start, the sooner you'll finish."

Skipper did his favorite trick of wiggling his left ear and raising his right eyebrow up and down at the same time, but he didn't argue any more.

"I don't even know where Johnstown is," Warren told Betsy.

"I think it's in Pennsylvania. Let's go to the library after school." Whispering, she mimicked Mr. Munson. "The sooner we start, the sooner we'll finish."

That afternoon Warren and Betsy checked out three books about the Johnstown flood from the public library. The librarian, Mrs. Vesper, said, "You should talk to Doc Keeton. His parents lived in Johnstown at the time of the flood. He may know some stories that have been passed down in his family that aren't in any of the published accounts."

"How can we contact him?" Betsy asked.

"I can't give out a patron's address or phone number," Mrs. Vesper said, "but I will call him and tell him of your interest in the flood. Then he can call you if he wants to."

"That would be great," Warren said. "Mr. Munson loves it when we get information that isn't in a book."

"He always tells us to seek unusual sources," Betsy said.

"Doc Keeton is definitely unusual," Mrs. Vesper said.

As they walked home, Warren said, "I hope Doc Keeton calls. It's so much easier to write a report when we have lots of information."

"If all else fails," Betsy said, "we can always use the Instant Commuter to see the flood in person."

"I don't want to go back to 1889. Floods are dangerous."

"In ancient Egypt," Betsy said, "the people *wanted* the Nile River to flood every year. That's how their farmlands got water."

"Johnstown," said Warren, "was not a farm."

CHAPTER

2

Rain. Tilda Minnigan had fallen asleep listening to rain on the roof, and she awoke to the same sound. What a spring. Would it ever end? Tilda wondered. Or was 1889 going to be the year it rained clear through the summer?

She stretched her legs, dumping Wags off her bed in the process. She dressed quickly and sloshed down the path to the outhouse, calling the reluctant dog to follow. Wags didn't like the rain any more than she did.

Back in the kitchen, she hurried to empty the nearly full buckets she kept on the floor, where the roof leaked.

George had already put wood on the fire. Grateful for the warmth, Tilda started heating water for the oatmeal. She took pride in sending her brother off to work with a good, hot breakfast and a full dinner pail.

Our last meal together for three whole months, Tilda thought. She hoped George would fix a hearty breakfast for himself while she was gone. At sixteen he was still growing, and he worked long, hard hours at the Cambria mill. But she knew he was more likely to grab a crust of bread than to fry an egg or boil some grain.

For a fleeting moment Tilda wondered if she had made the right choice. It would be terribly hard on George to be by himself for the whole summer, with no one to cook and scrub and wash the clothes.

At first George had not wanted her to accept the position as summer nursemaid for Mr. Robart's three little boys. "There's work enough for you here," he said, "and you're too young to leave home."

George was only one year older than Tilda, but he sometimes talked as if he were her parent.

"I need to get away from Johnstown for a time," Tilda said.

"What's wrong with Johnstown?"

"Nothing is wrong with Johnstown, but I have this yearning to know more, to see beyond this one city."

George shook his head, not understanding.

"You go off to the mill each day and talk with others," Tilda said. "You've found a way to support us, and in the process you've become a man. But I'm still like a little girl, living here in the same house we were born in, with only memories and neighbors to keep me company. I want to learn how other people live. I want to see different places and meet new people with fresh ideas."

And when I come home in September, she added to herself, I'll have money enough to fix the roof. My own money, earned, for the first time, by my own labor.

In the end George had agreed—partly, Tilda suspected, because he could see she was going to go to Altoona whether he approved or not.

When Mr. Robart sent her train ticket, he also sent a letter saying that they would spend the summer at his cottage on Lake Conemaugh.

"I envy you," George had said, "living up there in the mountains. Nothing to do all day long but dabble your toes in the lake and make hollyhock boats for the babies."

"Nothing to do?" Tilda said. "Those 'babies' are five, seven, and eight years old and probably as wild as wolves. I'm supposed to see that they do their lessons, read to them daily from The Holy Bible, and supervise their play. No doubt they'll run me ragged."

"I hear their nursemaid last summer quit after one week. Came screaming down out of the hills with her apron in tatters, and claimed she'd sooner work in the mines than go back for an hour with those undisciplined hoodlums."

"Who told you that?" Tilda demanded. Then, seeing the twinkle in George's eyes, she had realized he was teasing.

As Tilda spooned oatmeal into their bowls, plus some for Wags in a tin pie plate, George dripped into the kitchen, shaking droplets of water from his rubber raincoat.

The Flood Disaster

"You can quit worrying that I'll forget to weed the garden while you're away," he said. "The beans and corn are going to float off, and some lucky farmer in Florence will find plants growing where he never put seed."

"When the sun shone yesterday for the Memorial Day parade, I thought at last the rain was done, but it came down so hard in the night, it woke me twice."

"It had eased some when I got up, but now the sky is as black as coal, and as soon as you step outside, you can hear the rivers."

Wags licked his pie plate into a corner and kept licking it, making it clatter on the floor. Tilda picked it up and added some oatmeal from her own bowl.

"Be sure to feed Wags twice a day," she said.

"Fool dog. I wish you could take him with you. He'll probably howl all night."

Tilda smiled. "If he howls, let him get on your bed. That always quiets him."

"That is the reason he howls," George said. "He knows if he makes enough racket you'll reward him by letting him sleep with you."

Tilda laughed, knowing that George loved the little terrier as much as she did.

George finished his oatmeal and stood up. "I wish I could see you to the depot," he said.

"I can manage by myself."

"Well, goodbye, then," George said. "Safe journey." He put out his hand, but Tilda flung her arms around him and they clung together for a moment, the way they had after Mummy and Papa died.

When he was gone, Tilda quickly baked a shepherd's pie for George's supper. As she was cleaning the kitchen, George came back.

"When I got to the mill," he said, "the whole seven o'clock shift was told to go home and tend to our families. The rivers are rising fast, and some folks have water in their cellars already."

"I hope the train isn't delayed," Tilda said.

"We should go to the depot early so we can hear any reports."

The Flood Disaster

At nine o'clock Tilda gave Wags one last pat, then donned her coat and bonnet.

George hoisted her wicker trunk to one shoulder and opened the door.

Tilda walked carefully, trying to pick her way around the deepening puddles. She didn't want to ruin her good shoes.

A neighbor, Mr. Percy, passed them, leading his cow to higher ground. "I hear Main Street's under water," Mr. Percy said. "As soon as I tie my cow up the hill, I'm going to move all my furniture to the second story. People say the South Fork dam is close to breaking."

"People say that every spring," George replied.

"True, true," said Mr. Percy, "and the dam always holds."

They walked on. A family that they knew from church came along the side street, toting a suitcase.

"Are you taking the train, too?" Tilda asked.

"We're moving to the Hulbert House," the mother replied. "We feel we'll be safer at the hotel than in our house if the dam breaks."

When the family was out of earshot, George said, "Every year there are rumors that the dam is going to break, and every year people move from their homes to the Hulbert House, and every year nothing happens."

"Perhaps the hotel owners start the rumors."

Along Main Street, shop owners hustled to move their goods to the highest shelves where, they hoped, the water would never reach. A group of children, wet to the knees, floated small boxes in the widening puddles, pretending to have boat races.

Tilda gave up trying to keep her shoes dry. As she and George sloshed toward the station, the two rivers that converged in Johnstown, the Stony Creek and the Little Conemaugh, roared in the background, a constant reminder that the steady rain which pelted the town had no place to go. With more than one hundred days of rain or snow already that year, the sodden ground could hold no more.

A small crowd milled around the platform at the train station. Tilda asked the stationmaster about the train she was to take, the Day Express.

"It left Pittsburgh at eight-ten," he told her, "and we expect it to arrive in Johnstown on time, around ten-fifteen."

"I'm taking the Day Express to Altoona," she said.

"I wish I were going with you," he replied. "Far better to be above the dam today, than below it."

Tilda paced restlessly along the platform. The damp hem of her best dress swished about her ankles. At the west edge of the platform, she peered down the tracks before she headed back to George, who waited beside Tilda's trunk.

"Don't be so impatient for the train to arrive," George said. "People will think you are eager to leave home."

Tilda smiled at him. "I am eager to leave home," she said, then hastily added, "but not because of you, of course."

"Of course."

A shrill whistle pierced the thick wetness, and Tilda jumped at the sudden sound.

"Here she comes," said George.

Tilda stopped pacing, suddenly overcome with nervousness about the journey ahead of her.

"Perhaps I shouldn't go," she said. "Mr. Robart would surely understand if I don't come in the midst of flooding. I could ask Reverend Thompson to telephone him, and explain that I had to put off my travel for a day or two."

"If the rivers flood, they'll do it whether you stay or not," George said, "and there's nothing we can do except wait and watch. We have no second story to move to."

"I don't like to think of you and Wags by yourselves. What if the water reaches our house? It came nearly to our porch steps last year."

"If the water gets too high, I'll take Wags up in the hills and camp out a night or two. We'll have ourselves a good adventure."

The train chugged into view.

Tilda nervously smoothed her skirt. "I don't want to start my first day of employment with Mr. Robart by not taking the train after he purchased my ticket. He would think me undependable. But I worry about you and Wags. What if the dam really breaks?"

"We'll watch the excitement from Green Hill," George said. "And you'll be drier in Altoona than here."

Smoke filled the air and the steel wheels screeched as the train clanged to a stop.

Tilda stood still, torn between her desire to begin her summer job and her wish to be with George if there was serious flooding. She didn't want to be safe in Altoona if George was not safe here in Johnstown. Yet she knew that staying home would not prevent trouble. The weather was out of her hands.

George carried Tilda's trunk to the baggage car; Tilda followed.

"All aboard!" cried the conductor.

Tilda and George hurried to the front passenger car.

"I'll miss you," Tilda said.

"I'll miss you, too."

They hugged briefly once more, both aware that they were alone in the world except for each other.

"Go home now," she said, "and dry out by the fire. And promise you'll take Wags to high ground if the rivers reach our house."

Eagerness wrestled with reluctance in Tilda's heart as she boarded the train.

"Goodbye," George called. "I'll see you in September."

CHAPTER

3

The day after Warren and Betsy went to the library, Warren answered the phone and heard a scratchy voice say, "I hear you want to know about the flood."

"Doc Keeton?"

"When can you come over?" the voice asked.

"Would tomorrow after school be all right?"

"Yes, as long as you leave before my knitting class arrives. They come at five."

"We can be there by three-thirty," Warren said. "What's your address?"

Doc Keeton gave some fast directions

that concluded with "Look for the red goose." He hung up without saying goodbye.

The house proved easy to find. A large red tin sign in the shape of a goose hung near the front door. The sign, which looked old, said RED GOOSE SHOES.

Doc Keeton opened the door. Leaning on a cane, the wrinkled old man led Warren and Betsy into a large room that was crowded with dolls. Dolls were stacked on every piece of furniture; heaps of dolls and overflowing boxes of doll clothes filled the corners.

A long table in the center of the room contained arms, legs, heads, and other doll parts plus a box filled with glass eyes.

"I'm the doll doctor," Doc Keeton said. "Folks give me old dolls, I fix them up, and they're given to needy children at holiday time."

Shelves lined two walls. Betsy and Warren walked past them, admiring row after row of beautifully restored dolls.

"Those are finished," Doc Keeton said, "and ready for Santa to pick them up."

"They look brand-new," Warren said.

The Flood Disaster

Betsy put her fingertip on the cheek of a baby doll that wore an embroidered white dress. "This one looks as if it should be in a museum," Betsy said. "Is it old?"

"Not as old as I am," Doc said. "Every year on my birthday, I make up a poem that becomes my motto for the year. This year it's *Ninety-five and still alive.*"

"You don't look ninety-five," Betsy said.

"I'm aiming for *Ninety-nine and feeling fine.*"

"Why not *One-oh-one and having fun!*" Betsy asked.

"One-oh-two and never blue," said Warren.

Doc Keeton grinned at them. "I like you two," he said. "What do you want to know about the flood?"

"Anything you can tell us," Warren said.

"Do you mind if I work while we talk? If I don't keep my hands busy, I feel I'm wasting time, and at my age I don't have a lot of time left."

"May we help you?" Betsy asked.

Doc Keeton turned on a small iron and asked Betsy to iron a stack of doll clothes. He gave Warren a glass jar filled with buttons and asked him to sort them by color and put each color in a separate plastic bag.

Doc began sewing a new leg for a one-legged rag doll. As they worked, he talked:

"My mother and father and my sister, Anna, lived in Johnstown at the time of the flood. Anna was eight years old and an only child. She died that day—swept right out of my mother's arms into the water and washed away.

"I never knew her, of course. I didn't come along until many years later. My parents left Johnstown a few weeks after the flood. They had lost everything and wanted to escape the memories.

"They came as far west as they could and never went back. My mother would not talk about the flood or even about Anna, but my father told me what happened."

Doc finished the rag doll leg and hunted through one of the boxes of clothing for a dress to put on the doll. He handed the dress to Betsy to be pressed.

"My parents," he continued, "were not together when the flood hit Johnstown. My father worked as a logger then, and he was an hour's walk from town, up on one of the hills. He had started chopping early that morning, working in the rain, because he had not worked at all the day before. He had watched the Memorial Day parade with my mother and Anna.

"Mother and Anna were home when the water started to rise. It came in the house, covering the floor and climbing up the furniture. Mother and Anna mounted the ladder to the garret. Today we'd call it an attic. It was an unfinished room, with one small window.

"The water followed them to the garret. Inch by inch, it grew deeper until they stood with their heads pressed against the roof and the water touching their chins."

Betsy and Warren exchanged horrified glances as the story continued.

"Mother knew they would surely die if they remained, so she broke open the window, clutched Anna in her arms, and jumped out. The impact of the water jolted Anna out of Mother's grasp. As the flood carried Anna away, Mother scrambled on to the roof of a barn that floated past. She rode that barn roof for twelve hours, until she was finally rescued over in Kernville.

She and my father were reunited the next week, but Anna was never found."

"How awful," Betsy said.

"My father had two great sorrows that stayed with him his entire life. One was losing Anna. The other was the fact that Anna never got the doll she longed for. My parents were poor then, barely able to put food on the table, and when Anna begged for a doll that she saw in the general store, they could not buy it for her.

"Every time she went in the store, Anna gazed longingly at the doll. When the understanding shopkeeper tried to distract her with a free piece of penny candy, Anna thanked him politely and returned to the doll.

"The Christmas before the flood, Anna believed that Santa would bring the doll to her. When it didn't happen, she cried and cried and my mother cried, too. My father said it nearly broke his heart that he could not give his beloved child the one plaything she wanted.

"After they moved west and I was born, my father started a successful shoe store, which I later ran. But every year on Christmas morning, his eyes filled with tears and he said, 'Now that I can afford ten dolls, I have no little girl to give them to.'

"He described the doll to me so many times that even though I never saw it, I knew exactly what it looked like. It was made in Germany, with a cloth body and a bisque head. It was a young girl doll, wearing a pleated print dress and a bonnet. She had long reddish blond hair."

As he talked, Doc Keeton walked to one of the shelves that held the finished dolls. He took a box from the top shelf, opened it, and folded back several layers of tissue paper. Then he lifted out a doll that matched his description perfectly.

"This doll was given to me six years ago," he said, "and I knew immediately that it is exactly the doll that Anna wanted. I restored it as soon as I got it, but I can never bring myself to give it away. Whenever I take it from the shelf, I get the strangest feeling that I need to keep it for Anna. And so I do."

He rewrapped the doll and put the box back on the shelf.

"After I became a father myself," he continued, "I finally understood my own father's grief. That's when I started repairing the dolls. Making other children happy with a doll is a way to make up for the fact that my father could not give Anna the doll she wanted."

"How do you distribute them?" Warren asked.

"There used to be a large stone building at the edge of town called the Orphans' Home. Children who had no parents lived there. For many years my wife and son worked on the dolls with me, and every December we'd take all the dolls that we'd fixed that year and give them to the Orphans' Home. It was my memorial to my father, and to the sister I never knew.

"Now the Orphans' Home is gone, and so I give the dolls to the Salvation Army. They distribute them to needy children."

"It's a wonderful memorial," Betsy said.

"My only regret is that I never saw a picture of Anna. My father described her to me many times, but that isn't the same as a photograph. I've always wished I could see exactly what my sister looked like."

Betsy thought of her own sister. It would

be terrible not to have a single picture of Lori.

"Now my wife and son are both gone, too," Doc Keeton said, "and I just keep on mending dolls." He paused a moment and then said, "Now, isn't this a fine kettle of fish? You come here to learn about the flood, and I bore you with my family history."

"We aren't bored," Warren said.

"It's a fascinating story," Betsy said. "You must have made thousands of children happy with your gifts."

"I like to think so," Doc Keeton said.

"And we learned about the flood, too," Warren said.

"It's nearly five," Doc Keeton said. "I hate to chase you off, but my knitting group will be here soon. We meet once a month for potluck, and then we knit doll sweaters."

"Thanks for letting us come," Betsy said.

As Betsy and Warren walked home, Betsy said, "Maybe we could give Doc Keeton his wish."

"What do you mean?"

"We could use the Instant Commuter to go to Johnstown in 1889. We could carry a camera with us, find Anna, and take a picture of her. When we get home, we'll develop the film and give the picture to Doc Keeton."

"How would we explain where we got a picture of Anna? We can't tell him about the Instant Commuter."

"We wouldn't explain. We wouldn't even let Doc Keeton know that the picture was from us. We could just write *Anna* on the back and mail it to him. He would know from his father's description that it was really her."

"An anonymous gift."

"He's been giving anonymous gifts for years," Betsy said. "He deserves to receive one."

"How would we find Anna?"

"We know her name. Johnstown was a small town then; we'll just go to Johnstown and ask. It should be easy."

"An Instant Commuter trip," said Warren, "is never easy."

CHAPTER

Tilda found a window seat and nodded politely at the elderly woman who sat facing her.

She pressed her nose to the window, trying to see through the water that streamed down the outside of the glass. She saw George on the platform, waving.

"Goodbye!" Tilda mouthed the word, knowing George could not hear her. Waving, she watched him turn and head for home.

She sat back and wiped a tear from her cheek.

"A sad parting?" asked the white-haired woman in the opposite seat.

"Not really," Tilda said. "It's just that I've never been away from home before, and my brother, George, will be all on his own for the summer."

"Orphans are you, then?" asked the woman.

Tilda nodded. "Our parents died of the plague last year," she said. "Mummy first, and Papa two days after."

"My sympathy, dear," said the woman. "I lost a son to the plague and another in the war." She leaned forward and patted Tilda's arm. "One never forgets them," she said softly. "Never."

The conductor entered the car and announced, "There'll be a delay in our departure. The eastbound track farther up the valley has washed out."

"How long of a delay?" a man asked.

"I can't say exactly," the conductor replied. "We have men up there now, taking a look."

As nervous as she was about the train ride, and as anxious as she was about the possibility of a flood, Tilda did not want to stay another minute in Johnstown. Now that she'd said her goodbye to George, she could barely wait to meet her three young charges. And whenever she thought of the cottage at Lake Conemaugh, she bubbled with anticipation.

Mr. Robart had sent a photograph showing the cottage and the shoreline. Looking at the photo for the first time, Tilda didn't know which was more amazing: the fact that a new instrument called a Kodak camera could actually reproduce on paper what a person's eyes were seeing—or the fact that she, Tilda Minnigan, had been asked to spend the summer in such an elegant-looking place.

The word *cottage* seemed a misnomer to Tilda, since the white frame structure was three stories high, with a broad front porch and fancy carved trim.

"You won't want to come home," George had said when he saw the photo.

But she would, Tilda knew. Her home was in Johnstown with George and Wags, and she missed them already.

Still she was eager to leave. She intended to look hard and listen carefully, and soak up every new event in the three months ahead.

When she returned home, she would no longer be an inexperienced and sheltered fifteen-year-old; she would be a mature young woman who had traveled by train and lived on a lake and earned her own keep.

The passengers sat in silence for a moment. Then the old woman across from Tilda said, "My name is Mrs. Dopkins."

"I'm Tilda Minnigan. I'm going to Altoona, to be nursemaid for the summer to three little boys."

"How lovely," said Mrs. Dopkins. "A summer with young children will raise your spirits."

"I'm a trifle nervous," Tilda confessed. "I've not had much experience with little ones. I suspect I got the job only because the minister of my church, Reverend Thompson, played on the heartstrings of the boys' father, painting me as a virtuous, hardworking person in need of financial assistance."

"If that description is accurate," said Mrs. Dopkins, "and I trust that it is, you will have no trouble as a nursemaid. I'll give you a hint for getting along well with lively little boys: respect and enjoy them, and they will live up to your high expectations."

"Where are you headed?" Tilda asked.

"Cresson. My daughter and her family are there, and I'm going to stay with them. I pray I won't be a burden to Ruth. With seven little ones, she doesn't need another mouth to feed. I hope to be of some use to her. Due to the gout in my leg, I need aid getting around, but I can still rock a baby and do mending."

"I'm sure your help will be appreciated," Tilda said.

Mrs. Dopkins leaned forward, her eyes glowing with excitement. "Ruth and Clarence have electricity," she said. "And next year they hope to get an indoor bathroom."

"Will they be meeting you at the station?" Tilda asked.

"Oh, yes. Even with my cane I need help to walk. Ruth will meet me, and probably her two oldest boys as well. They'll bring a spring buggy to carry my things. Fancy it: electric lights in Ruth's kitchen!"

"My employer has one of those telegraph instruments right in his home," Tilda said.

"Gracious," said Mrs. Dopkins. "He must be a man of considerable financial means."

"He's an official with the Pennsylvania Railroad. He uses the telegraph to check on weather conditions."

"Times are changing," Mrs. Dopkins said. "I've heard there are already seventy telephones right here in Johnstown, and Clarence predicts that one day every house will have indoor plumbing."

"I hope he's right," Tilda said. "Those dark walks down the path at night are horrid, especially in winter."

Through the rain-streaked windows, Tilda saw a boy she knew. He was leaning out of a second-floor window across from the depot, waving at someone below.

Two men who were seated across the aisle from Tilda left the train for a few minutes. When they came back, they reported that a crew of railroad men were working to dislodge logs and drift from the stone bridge.

"I've never seen the river this high," one of them said.

Half an hour after the conductor's initial

announcement, he returned. "We're ready to depart," he said.

"The track's been repaired already?" Mrs. Dopkins asked.

"No. We're going to run east on the west-bound track," the conductor said. "We'll follow a local mail train, to ensure your safety."

The train chugged slowly away from Johnstown. When it rounded the corner of Prospect Hill, Tilda looked out the window and gasped. The Little Conemaugh River surged forward, very near the tracks.

Whole trees rode the dirty, yellow-brown water. Fence posts, broken boards, and other debris tumbled into view and passed almost before she could make out what they were.

"Look how fast the river is flowing," Tilda said.

Mrs. Dopkins nodded.

Only ten minutes after leaving Johnstown, the Day Express stopped in East Conemaugh. Once again the conductor delivered bad news.

"There's been trouble up the line at Lilly. Bear Run rose more than six feet, over-flowed its banks, and washed out a quarter of a mile of track. All trains are being held here in East Conemaugh."

"For how long?" asked the same man who had asked how long they'd be delayed in Johnstown.

"I have no way to know that," said the conductor.

Tilda wondered why some people ask questions that clearly have no answer. How could the conductor possibly know how long the rain would continue, or when the river might stop raging across the land where the tracks had been, or how long it would take to replace the washed-out tracks?

"Ruth will be worried sick about me," Mrs. Dopkins said. "We could be detained here for hours."

I should have stayed with George, thought Tilda. This isn't a typical spring flood, as we've had in past years. This is worse. Much, much worse.

George waded across Main Street, not caring that the water now climbed over the tops of his shoes and splashed around his ankles. He looked back once, when the Day

The Flood Disaster

Express pulled away from the station platform. He watched seven train cars—five
coaches, one baggage car, and a sleeping
car—chug east away from Johnstown. They
were followed by a second section of the
Day Express, but George turned away as
soon as Tilda's car was out of sight.

He didn't like this. He didn't like it one
bit. From the beginning he had been against
having Tilda leave for the summer to work
as a nursemaid, although he had to admit
her reasons for doing so were sound. And
once he had adjusted to the notion, he was
rather proud of his sister for having the
gumption to go off to Altoona and earn her
own wages.

But he didn't like having her travel today
when the rain threatened to flood not only
the rivers, but the entire town. Who would
watch out for Tilda if the train tracks
washed out? What would she do if she was
unable to reach her destination? She had no
money for food or lodging.

What if there was flooding in Altoona
and Mr. Robart was unable to meet the
train, to escort Tilda to his home? What if
the tracks washed away and the engineer

on the Day Express didn't see it in time?

I should not have allowed her to go, George thought. Yet how could I have stopped her?

He paused in front of the dry-goods store and peered in the window. Inside, the owner was moving all his merchandise to the top shelves.

Wagons rattled past on the street, loaded with families seeking higher ground. George heard one of the drivers call out to a friend, "Get out of Johnstown! The dam is going to break, and you'll be swept away."

"You told me that last year," the friend responded, "and the year before that."

It was true, George thought. Every spring when the rivers overflowed their banks, doomsayers warned that the dam would burst and all in its path would drown. George had heard the warnings every year, as far back as he could remember. Yet it had never happened, and he saw no reason to think it would happen this time.

Still, he decided to get Wags and climb up into the hills above town. It would be better than sitting in the lonely house, listening to the rain fill the buckets in the kitchen while he worried about Tilda.

He and Wags could find a spot under a tree and share the shepherd's pie that Tilda had baked for him that morning. Perhaps someone would offer to let him use a tent or other temporary shelter.

George hurried home and hastily added the shepherd's pie to the dinner Tilda had packed for him that morning. There was plenty of food to last until tomorrow.

He took the blanket from his bed and rolled it up with his other pair of pants and some dry stockings inside. He put on a second shirt, right over the one he was wearing, then slipped back into his raincoat. He wished he had a way to keep the rolled blanket dry.

"Come, Wags," he said, and he headed for the door. At the last minute he turned back, took his parents' framed wedding certificate off the table, and stuffed it into the center of his bedroll.

Just in case, George told himself. If the water should rise higher than other years and flood the entire house, the memento his parents had cherished would be safe.

He took one last look around. There was nothing else of value in the house.

"Come, Wags," George said.

With the little terrier at his side, he went out the door, surprised by how much the water had risen in the short time he had been inside. It was over the porch steps already. At that rate Stony Creek must be rising more than a foot an hour.

When he put his foot on solid ground, the water came halfway to his knees. Wags stood on the porch, feet firmly planted, unwilling to plunge into the cold, brown water.

"I don't blame you," George muttered. "It'll be over your head in no time."

Wishing Tilda were with him, George scooped the dog into his arms and splashed away from home, toward the hills.

CHAPTER

5

"If we plan carefully," Betsy said, "we can go to Johnstown, take a picture of Anna, and come home again with no problem." She and Warren were sitting on Betsy's front step with Betsy's current foster dog, Empress.

"We planned carefully before we went to see the blizzard," Warren said, "and we nearly froze to death."

Betsy continued to brush Empress. "Good dog," she said. "Good Empress."

"That's a fancy name for a dog who's less than a foot tall," Warren said, trying to get off the subject of the Instant Commuter.

He wanted to surprise Doc Keeton with a photo of Anna, but he didn't want to have to go to Johnstown in order to do it.

"Pekingese dogs were special to the Chinese emperors. For centuries the Imperial Court gave all Pekingese the sacred standing of Lion Dog of China. Their pedigrees were painted on silk screens."

"Does Empress have a pedigree?"

"No. She was released to the Purebred Dog Rescue by a neighbor of her owner. The owner moved and left Empress behind without making any arrangement for her care. Can you believe it? He just locked her in an empty house and left. How can people be so irresponsible? How can they be so—"

"Don't get started," Warren said. "I already agree with you."

"The neighbor had always been told that Empress was a purebred Pekingese, but there were no papers to prove it, and no way to contact the owner."

"Will that hurt her chances of getting adopted?"

"Not really. Most of the people who want to adopt a dog from our group are looking for a companion, not a show animal. Usually they want a particular breed because they've had that breed in the past and think it's the best kind of dog in the world."

"She looks as if she walked into a wall and squashed her nose flat," Warren said.

"Now about Johnstown," said Betsy. "If we go there with a camera, we can take other pictures in addition to the one of Anna."

Warren opened his mouth to protest, but Betsy rushed on.

"The pictures we found in books," she said, "were all taken several days after the flood. Cameras were not common back then, and with the train tracks washed out, it took awhile for photographers to get to Johnstown after word of the flood got out."

"True. Anyone in Johnstown who did have a camera was probably too busy trying to save himself to think about photographs."

"After we get the picture of Anna, we can use up the rest of the film taking pictures of the flood. When we get home and have the film developed, we'll have the only actual pictures of an important historical event."

Although he still didn't want to travel to the flood in person, Warren was intrigued by Betsy's idea. "Do you think we could develop the film just like normal, even though the pictures were taken in 1889?"

"Why not? Think how exciting this would be for historians. We can give the pictures to the Johnstown Flood Museum that we found on the Internet. They'll be thrilled."

"We would have to explain how we got the pictures, which would mean letting the world know about the Instant Commuter."

Betsy thought a moment. "We'll send the photos anonymously, the same as we're going to do with the picture of Anna."

"The lab that develops the film would know who brought it in."

Betsy quit brushing Empress and cleaned the fur out of the brush. Empress promptly flopped on her back and rolled in the grass.

"Maybe we shouldn't hide the Instant Commuter any longer," Betsy said. "Maybe you should patent it and sell it to a company that would manufacture it. If we explain how we got the flood pictures, it would be fantastic publicity for the Instant Commuter. You'll probably be on the *Today* show. You'll end up a billionaire and won't want to hang out with me anymore."

"I can't quit hanging out with you. How would I learn the truth about fireflies and glowworms and sacred dogs in ancient China?"

Betsy smiled. "Shall we go back to Johnstown and take pictures of the flood as it happens?"

"No," Warren said. "Even if I wanted to do it, which I don't, we can't. The Instant Commuter's probe has to touch a photo before it can transport us through time to that place. Since there are no photographs of the actual flood, there's no way for the Instant Commuter to take us there during the flood."

"I thought of that," Betsy said. "We'll have to try an experiment."

"I don't think I want to hear this," Warren said.

"When we first used the Instant Commuter, we thought it would only work on a map. Then we discovered it works on photographs, too. This time let's try it with a drawing. There are plenty of sketches of the flood. Maybe the Instant Commuter will work on one of those."

"I wonder if it would work."

"We can carefully choose the spot on the drawing that the probe touches, so we don't end up in the water. We could stand high on a hill, or we can pick one of the buildings that we know survived, such as that stone Methodist Church."

Warren hesitated. Real pictures of such a famous event would be of great interest to many people. And he did want to surprise Doc Keeton.

"We'll put the Instant Commuter in a heavy plastic bag to keep it dry," Betsy said.

"The Instant Commuter isn't a toy," Warren said. "I've thought about this a lot since the blizzard disaster, and I believe that the capability to travel back in time is so special that it should be used only for important reasons."

He leaned down and scratched Empress behind her ears. "A desire to get photos of the flood doesn't qualify as an important reason, and neither does the wish to help Doc Keeton."

"I totally agree," Betsy said.

"You do?"

"Absolutely."

"Then why are you suggesting that we try to use a drawing as a way to travel back to the flood?"

"Maybe we can change the outcome. Maybe we can save some lives."

"I tried to do that when Mount Saint Helens was going to erupt. I told people that the volcano was going to blow, and they looked at me like I was crazy. The same thing would happen in Johnstown if we try to warn them."

"Maybe not."

"The people in Johnstown ignored the warnings that they got at the time. Even when a telegraph came into Johnstown from the site of the dam, saying the dam was about to break, the people didn't pay any attention. They had heard the same prediction year after year and it had never actually happened, so they didn't think it would happen that time, either. If they wouldn't listen to their own authorities, they surely won't listen to us."

"But what if they did?" Betsy said. "What if we could convince people to evacuate their homes and go to higher ground? We would save their lives."

"You're talking about going back in time and changing history. I'm not so sure we should try to do that."

"Why not, if it would help people?"

"It seems like trying to be God, or going against Nature, or something."

" 'Do unto others as you would have others do unto you,' " Betsy said. "What about the little kids?"

Warren thought about it. In the books he had read about the flood, there were many accounts of children who were swept away and drowned. Others became trapped in the debris that washed against the railroad bridge, and burned to death when the debris caught fire. Little kids couldn't be blamed for not heeding the warnings. What if he and Betsy could save some of them? What if they could save Anna?

"I started a list of what we should take

with us," Betsy said. She handed Warren a piece of yellow tablet paper.

Camera and extra film
Matches and newspaper, in case
  Instant Commuter gets wet
Life jackets for us
Life preserver to throw to others

"Do you have life jackets?" Warren asked.

"Yes. Mom and Dad bought four of them when we rented a cabin one summer on Sun Lake. We wore them when we went water skiing."

Betsy tied a blue ribbon on Empress's collar and made a big bow. "We have a life preserver, too. It's one of those round white rings, on the end of a rope. We'll toss it to people, and then they can hang on while we pull them out of the water."

Empress scratched at the bow with her hind leg until she got it untied. Then she clamped her teeth on the ribbon and tried to pull it off.

"All right, all right," Betsy said as she

removed the ribbon. "You don't have to wear a bow."

"I wonder if we *could* change history," Warren said.

"There's only one way to find out," Betsy replied. She threw a tennis ball; Empress chased it.

"I've figured out a better way to come home, too," Betsy continued. "Instead of using the map and taking a chance that we'll land where people will see us, we'll take a Polaroid picture of my backyard, just before we leave. When we're ready to return, we'll put the probe on the picture."

"Good idea." Warren added *Picture of Betsy's yard* to Betsy's list. If he was going to travel back to 1889, he wanted to be positive he could come home again.

CHAPTER

6

Tilda wished she had stayed home with George. Three hours after the train stopped in East Conemaugh, it was still there.

Tilda got off once with some of the other passengers and crossed the railroad tracks to the bank of the river.

A large group of people milled around on the riverbank, watching the torrent rush past. Two young men used rakes to fish items out of the water. It became a sport, with the crowd cheering when one of them successfully retrieved a wooden bench.

Tilda watched awhile, amused by the car-

51

nival atmosphere in the midst of such a dilemma. Her amusement faded when she realized that in the short time she had stood on the riverbank, the water had risen sharply. The wooden bridge near the station looked as if it would wash away at any moment.

Thoroughly drenched, she returned to the train and reported what she had seen to Mrs. Dopkins. "If the river continues to rise, the track we are on will soon be flooded," Tilda said.

Seconds later the train whistle gave a short blast. As soon as all the passengers had scrambled back on board, the Day Express moved slowly forward.

"Thank goodness," Mrs. Dopkins said. "We're on our way to Cresson at last."

"No," a porter corrected her. "We are staying here in East Conemaugh, but we're moving north toward the hill, to be farther from the water."

The train stopped again. Soon Tilda heard shouting from the area they had left. Curious, she got off and looked back at the place where the Day Express had been sitting. The river was quickly eroding away the dirt under the tracks.

Tilda stared as the earth crumbled from beneath the tracks, leaving a gaping hole. Within minutes the heavy steel rails began to twist as if they were only thin wires, and the tracks fell into the water.

Tilda gasped and turned to the porter, who had disembarked, too. "If the train had not moved when it did," she said, "we would all be in the river."

"The yard master is watching from the tower," the porter said. "He directed the train to move from that track." He patted Tilda's arm. "Don't you worry, miss. The great Pennsylvania Railroad Company takes care of its patrons. You're safe with us."

Am I? Tilda wondered. True, the Day Express had moved farther up the hill in time, but the river seemed to be chasing it. A quick glance told her that the train was now on the last siding next to town. They could get no farther from the river.

For the first time she began to consider leaving the train. But where would she go? She knew no one in East Conemaugh. Even if she did, the residents there were in no position to take in a visitor; they were as threatened by the flood as the train was.

A cold wind blew the rain into her face as she looked across the muddy streets of the town.

"You'd best get out of that rain, miss," the porter said.

Tilda followed him back into the passenger car.

She took her seat near Mrs. Dopkins again. Mrs. Dopkins's eyes were closed, and her lips moved silently. Tilda wasn't certain if the old woman was praying or dreaming.

Filled with apprehension, Tilda peered out the window, watching and waiting. More than once she saw the train yard master leave his post and go to check the river.

The train did not move.

By 3:15, after waiting nearly five hours, Tilda's chin drooped to her chest and she dozed uneasily. She jerked awake, startled by the shrill blasts of a train whistle. The whistle kept blowing, and blowing, without letup.

The porter who had assured her she was safe ran down the aisle.

The Flood Disaster

"Why does the whistle keep blowing that way?" Tilda asked. "What does it mean?"

"It means trouble, miss."

"Has the dam broken?" Mrs. Dopkins asked.

"I don't know," the porter said, "but I think so. The engineer is trying to warn us."

Tilda jumped to her feet.

Outside the window, the conductor raced along the track shouting, "Get to the hill! Get to the hill!"

Mrs. Dopkins fumbled with her cane, trying to stand. Tilda grabbed the old woman's arm and pulled her upright.

Passengers crowded into the aisle, headed for the exit at the rear of the car. Even with Tilda's help, Mrs. Dopkins moved too slowly for those in the aisle behind them. A young man grasped Mrs. Dopkins around the waist, lifted her feet from the floor, and carried her in front of him the rest of the way through the car. When they reached the steps leading down to the platform, he set her down with a *thunk*, leaped from the steps, and ran off.

"Hurry!" Tilda said as Mrs. Dopkins inched forward toward the first step.

"You go on," Mrs. Dopkins said. "I'm too slow."

Tilda hesitated.

"Save yourself," Mrs. Dopkins said. "Run!"

"Hang on to me," Tilda said. "You'll go faster if you use me instead of your cane."

A woman with two small children who had been the first to exit the train now returned. "It's safer in there," the woman declared as she shepherded the children back up the steps. "The only way to reach the hill is to jump across a ten-foot-wide ditch filled with water over my boys' heads. We would never make it."

"Nor will I," said Mrs. Dopkins. She let go of Tilda. "Thank you for helping me," she said, "but I choose to stay on the train. If my life ends here, I have lived long and well. You are still young. Go. And God go with you."

Tilda whispered, "And with you," before she rushed down the steps to the muddy track. She heard a loud roar and thought for a moment that another train was approaching. She looked over her shoulder toward the sound, and her heart rose to her throat.

A black mist surged toward the train from the direction of the river. The noise came from behind the mist, where a huge heap of broken buildings moved toward her, pushed forward by the high water.

The wall of debris, higher than any structure Tilda had ever seen, moved rapidly toward East Conemaugh, flattening everything in its path.

Tilda raced in the opposite direction down the railroad track until she reached the back of the train. She went around it, toward town. Ahead of her she could see the street climbing the hill to higher ground, but between her and the street was the ditch the young mother had talked about.

A woman floundered in the ditch, with the water up to her armpits. Her cries for help mingled with the roar of the river. A gray-haired couple, holding hands, tried to leap across the ditch, and failed.

On the far side two men who had made

it safely across leaned down and helped the couple and the woman climb out.

Tilda teetered on the edge of the ditch.

The men on the far side looked up. One of them shouted, "Here it comes! Run for your life!"

Tilda backed up, got a running start, and jumped as far as she could. She landed just short of the other side.

As her feet started down into the murky brown water in the ditch, she clawed at the ground, desperately trying to climb out. Her fingers dug into the dirt, and she pulled herself up out of the ditch.

Ahead of her, the two men and those they had helped ran full speed up the hill. Behind her Tilda saw the mountain of debris surging toward her. It loomed over the train, at least forty feet high, and the roar of it filled her ears.

She raced up the hill faster than her legs had ever moved. She paused once to catch her breath and looked back just as the wall of water and debris hit the train.

The passenger car she had been in broke loose from the rest of the train. It bobbed down the river like the toy boats the children had floated in the streets of Johns-town. Tilda thought about Mrs. Dopkins and the others who had remained on the train.

In an instant the water rushed across the tracks and into the town. She heard loud cracking sounds as houses and businesses broke apart and crumbled into the water.

Stores flattened as if they were made of paper. Houses toppled, some rolling from side to side before they were swept away. Others collapsed as if a giant boot had stomped on them.

The ditch she had leaped over merged with the river and became a part of the torrent.

Horrified, Tilda turned away and ran farther up the hill.

The next time she looked down, the entire railroad yard was under water. Huge locomotives floated like corks on fishing lines. Even the enormous roundhouse, where the engines were kept when not in use, was demolished.

Most of the railroad track was gone, as well, and less than half the buildings in town remained standing. Tilda knew the river would now flow straight to Johnstown, carrying with it the broken buildings of East Conemaugh.

My home, she thought, will surely be destroyed. It stood in a lower part of town, well below the hill. Tears splashed down her already wet cheeks as she thought of the small frame house, the one thing of value that she and George had inherited from their parents. It would be gone now, and with it their only hope of a secure future.

Where would she and George live when this was over? How would they ever get the money for another house?

An even worse thought made her throat feel tight. What if George had not taken Wags to a safe place? What if he had decided to wait it out at home?

No, she told herself. He'd promised he would take Wags into the hills. But how far had he gone? Were they high enough to escape this unthinkable destruction? Or would the raging water filled with smashed buildings descend before they could escape?

Tilda shuddered. She could do nothing to help her brother or her dog. She could only pray for their safety and wonder when, or if, she would ever see them again.

CHAPTER

7

Warren lengthened the straps on the backpack that contained the Instant Commuter. "This doesn't fit too well over a life jacket," he said as he buckled the strap across his chest.

Betsy wore an orange life jacket, too. The white life preserver ring hung on one arm; in the other hand she had a plastic bag containing the camera, film, matches, paper, and a picture of her backyard.

Warren held the Instant Commuter probe in his hand. He looked at the drawing he and Betsy had selected. The drawing showed the main part of Johnstown, with shops, churches, and a few houses. People walked the streets, some going in and out of stores. In the background, the two rivers that converged at Johnstown neared the tops of their banks. The caption said, "Citizens ignore warnings."

If the Instant Commuter worked on the drawing, Betsy and Warren would soon be in Johnstown just before the flood.

"Be sure to touch the probe behind a building," Betsy said, "where we are not likely to be seen as we arrive. If we suddenly appear out of nowhere in front of people, we'll scare them out of their wits."

"We may anyway," Warren said. "We don't exactly look as if we belong in 1889. Especially you. All the women in these drawings are wearing long skirts, not pants."

"With my hair stuffed up under this cap, they'll think I'm a boy," Betsy said. "I'm ready. Are you?"

Warren took a deep breath, then blew it out. "Ready," he said.

Betsy stood behind Warren, with the front of her life jacket tight against his backpack. She put her arms around his life jacket, stretching so she could clasp her hands together in front of Warren.

"Do you want to count down?" Warren asked.

"No. Just do it, before I get more nervous."

Warren turned on the Instant Commuter, pointed the probe at a church in the drawing, and let the tip rest on an area behind the church.

The small box began vibrating. Warren put the drawing in his pocket.

"Here we go," Betsy said.

A strong wind blew across Warren and Betsy, as it always did when they traveled with the Instant Commuter.

"Hang on!" Warren said.

The wind increased until it was difficult to stand upright. Betsy and Warren closed their eyes and braced themselves.

A minute later the wind stopped, and they knew the journey was complete.

Betsy and Warren stood beside a large frame building. Mud oozed up the sides of their rubber boots and rain pelted their heads. They looked around; no one had seen them arrive.

"We should have worn raincoats," Warren said.

They went along the side of the building to the front and read the sign: ST. JOHN'S ROMAN CATHOLIC CHURCH. A tall spire with a cross on top reached heavenward. Smaller spires rose on each side of the entry.

"What a pretty church," Betsy said. "I wonder if it survived the flood."

They walked to the nearest house, their boots making a *schlup, schlup* sound as they sank into the mud. They knocked on the door, but no one answered.

They hurried to the next house; it was also unoccupied, but a man came around from the back side, leading a mule on a tether.

"We're looking for the Keeton family," Warren said.

The man squinted at them, as if trying to see them more clearly. "You from around these parts?" he asked.

"We're visiting," Betsy said.

"Thought so." He pointed at Warren's life jacket. "Them orange coats you two are wearing don't look none too warm."

"They float in water," Betsy said.

"That so? You worried about the dam breaking?"

"Yes."

"Picked an odd time to come calling, if you're worried about that."

"We need to find the Keetons."

"There's a Keeton lives down in the hollow," the man said, pointing to a row of identical houses in the distance. "Works at the mill with my brother."

"Thanks," Warren said. "We heard the dam's about to break. Maybe you should take your mule to higher ground."

"Where did you say you're from?" the man asked.

"Prospect," Betsy said, recalling the name of a nearby community.

"Them coats would be warmer if you put sleeves in 'em," the man said. "It may be the end of May, but it's still mighty chilly."

"Thanks for your help," Betsy said.

She and Warren hurried in the direction the man had pointed.

When Warren glanced back over his shoulder, he saw the man still standing in the street, staring after them. "If he tells anyone about two people wearing sleeveless orange coats that float, they'll think he's crazy," Warren said. "Especially when he says the people were from Prospect."

"I couldn't say we live in Issaquah, Washington. Washington was not yet an official state at the time of the flood."

Warren laughed. Who but Betsy the Human Encyclopedia would know the date of statehood?

They passed a few other people who looked at them curiously but who politely nodded and refrained from asking who they were.

Just before the street dipped down into what the man had called the hollow, Betsy and Warren saw the river a few blocks away. "There's the stone railroad bridge," Warren said.

"It makes me feel creepy," Betsy said, "to look at that bridge and know a lot of people who are walking around right now will soon die there."

The main part of town lay below them, with the river beyond it. The bridge was at the edge of the city, on their left. Hills on both sides of the river acted like a funnel, directing the water toward the bridge.

The Flood Disaster

Betsy and Warren hurried down the hill to the row of small frame houses. Betsy rapped on the door of the first one. A woman with a baby in her arms and a toddler clinging to her skirt opened the door.

"Excuse me," Betsy said. "We're looking for a little girl named Anna Keeton. Would you know where she lives?"

"Yonder," the woman replied. "The third house on the opposite side of the street. Anna goes to school with my Emily."

"Thank you," Betsy said. "Are you planning to take your children to higher ground soon? The water's getting deep fast."

"We have no shelter but this," the woman said. "If it gets too deep, we'll sit on the roof of the chicken house."

"That won't save you," Betsy said. "You need to climb up in the hills, as high as you can. And go quickly!"

The woman's eyes grew wide with concern at the urgency in Betsy's voice. "Perhaps you're right," she said.

Warren tugged on Betsy's sleeve and started toward the Keeton house.

"Good luck," Betsy told the woman as she followed Warren.

They paused at the Keeton house long enough for Betsy to take the camera out of the plastic bag and get it ready to use. Then Warren knocked on the door.

A small girl answered. She wore a dark green long-sleeved dress, with a white pinafore over it. Her blond hair was parted in the center and held back on each side with green ribbons.

"Are you Anna?" Betsy asked.

The girl nodded.

"My name is Betsy and I want to take your picture. Would that be all right?"

The child nodded again.

A voice from inside called, "Who is it, Anna?"

"Just stand still, right where you are," Betsy said as she stepped back a few feet. She quickly checked to be sure Anna was in the center of the camera's viewfinder, and then clicked the shutter. The flash went off.

"What was that?" Anna said, raising a hand to her eyes.

"Anna!" the voice said again. "Who is at the door?"

The Flood Disaster

"The light goes off when we take a picture," Warren explained.

Betsy took a second picture. The light flashed again.

A woman came to stand behind Anna. "Good day," she said.

"It won't be a good day if you stay here," Betsy blurted. "The dam's going to break, and your house will be washed away—and Anna with it."

Anna began to whimper.

"I'll thank you not to alarm my child with rumors," the woman said. "Who are you?"

"We only want to help you. If you leave now, you might be able to save Anna's life."

"My husband decides such matters," the woman said, "and he is not at home now."

"Please believe me," Betsy said. "Don't wait for your husband. If you do, you'll lose your only child."

The woman's eyes narrowed suspiciously. "How do you know Anna is my only child? Who are you?" She pointed to the camera. "What's in that odd box?"

"This is a camera," Warren said. "We are

friends of Doc Keeton, who lives in the west. He sent us because he is worried about your safety."

The woman snorted. "You have the wrong house," she said. "There are no doctors in the Keeton clan, only millworkers."

"Mama, am I going to drown in the flood?" Anna whispered.

"Such nonsense," her mother replied. "You are as safe as a butterfly in a meadow." She turned away from the doorway, ushering little Anna ahead of her. "Good day," she said over her shoulder.

Just before the door closed, a loud noise came from the direction of the river.

"It may be starting," Betsy said.

Mrs. Keeton hesitated, then shut the door.

CHAPTER

8

George's arms ached from carrying his bedroll, the dinner pail, and Wags. How could such a small dog seem so heavy?

Wags panted nervously, his tongue hanging out the side of his mouth. It was the way he always acted prior to a thunderstorm. Tilda swore Wags knew in advance when lightning and thunder were coming, and George had to admit the dog did seem to sense such storms before they hit.

"It's all right, Wags," George murmured as he struggled uphill with the dog in his arms. "You'll be safe with me."

When he finally reached a point where his feet were not under water, George let out a sigh of relief and put Wags on the ground. It still wasn't dry land—there was no such thing as dry land anywhere near Johnstown that day—but at least the water was not over George's shoes, or Wags's paws.

Wags, his tail tucked between his legs, shivered at George's feet. George wasn't sure if the dog shook from cold or fear, or both.

Other townsfolk struggled up the hill, pausing near George to catch their breath before continuing. Some carried baskets filled with food and clothing. Others pulled wagons of various sizes, piled with household belongings.

A man leading a donkey stopped next to George. The donkey raised its head and brayed.

Wags leaped into the air and ran toward home. Water splashed around him as he ran, but the little dog was too scared to care.

"Wags! Come back, Wags!"

George's shouts were ignored as the terrier tried to put as much distance as possible between himself and the donkey.

George wedged his rolled blanket into the crook of a large maple tree, then set the dinner pail on top of the blanket. Hoping he would be able to find them again, he took off after Wags.

The panic-stricken dog dodged around bushes and zigzagged back and forth as he tried to stay high enough to keep the water from creeping up his legs.

Behind him, George crashed through the shrubbery, still calling. Twice he caught a glimpse of the dog, so he knew he was going in the right direction, but the distance between them lengthened. Wags might be small, George thought, but he can run faster than I can.

George didn't like going back toward Johnstown. All the talk he had heard over the years of what would happen if the dam ever burst now crowded into his head. We should be running in the other direction, he thought, just in case.

Yet he had to try to catch Wags. Tilda doted on that dog as if it were a child. If anything happened to Wags, Tilda would be heartsick.

The water inched farther up the hill. George had to keep veering to his left in order to stay at the waterline.

He came to the crest of a small hill and saw Wags in the distance. Wags had stopped and was sniffing the air, as if trying to decide which way to turn.

"Wags!" George shouted. He raced toward the dog. "Wags!"

Wags heard the second shout. He turned to look at George. He moved a few feet toward George, then stopped and waited.

George scooped the soaking-wet dog into his arms. Just as he started away from town again, he heard a loud rumbling. Wags shook so hard that George's arms vibrated.

The rumbling grew louder, becoming a fast series of crashes that exploded one after the other like shots from a gun, only louder. Much, much louder. On the far side of town a train whistle blew and blew.

It's a warning, George realized. He turned and ran as fast as he could.

The noise followed him, growing louder until George could not sort out individual sounds inside the overall racket. Noises of buildings breaking apart and horses neighing and people shouting blended together in a symphony of terror.

He got a stitch in his side from running so hard, and paused to look back. He saw a wall of water, filled with smashed lumber, bearing down upon him. There was no way he could outrun it. George knelt in the mud, bending over Wags to protect him, and waited for the wave to hit.

It crashed over his head, carrying him forward at a dizzying rate. Trees were torn from the ground like weeds plucked from a garden and went whirling downstream. Gasping for air, and still clutching Wags under one arm, George saw half a small shed float past. He grabbed at the roof of the shed, cutting his hand on a strip of tin that ran along the roof's edge. He tried again, and that time he was able to grasp the edge of the roof and pull himself and Wags up onto it.

Together they crouched on the roof as the shed floated away. Wags's toenails scratched against the roof as he struggled to keep his footing.

A large sign floated past: IRON SLEDS SOLD HERE. George had not seen that sign before, and he wondered where it came from. Probably from one of the towns upstream, such as Woodvale or East Conemaugh, which was Tilda's destination. Were those towns washed out, too? What had happened to Tilda, and to the train she was riding?

A large tree, its branches twisted and torn, bumped into the shed. The jolt made him lose his grip on Wags, and the dog skidded down the shed roof toward the water.

George flung himself forward and grabbed Wags by the tail just before Wags slid off the edge. George braced his feet, digging his heels into the shingles, and pulled Wags backward up the roof.

George saw a cow near the shore, frantically trying to climb out of the water. The cow's front legs pawed at the riverbank. Before it could get its hooves stable, the flow pushed it downstream, where it tried again and again, until it was forced too far out in the river.

The cow was still swimming when George saw a cluster of people on the riverbank ahead. They waved and shouted at him, although he could not hear what they said. As he approached, he saw that the people on shore were going to throw him a rope.

George put one arm around Wags and pulled the dog close against him. He crouched, desperately trying to keep his balance as the shed bobbed and tilted in the river.

A man threw the rope at exactly the right moment. It landed on the shed roof. George crawled toward it, stretching his arm until his fingers closed around it.

The group on shore called out, encouraging him. They quickly lined up as if they were playing tug-of-war, and everyone pulled on the rope. As it went taut, George felt as if his arm would be pulled from the socket.

I need to hold on with both hands, George realized. I won't make it otherwise. But he couldn't hold on to the rope and Wags both. He would need to let go of Wags and leave the dog behind.

George had but a split second to make his choice: leave Wags, grip the rope with both hands, and get pulled to shore. Or let the rope go and remain with Wags, and hope to save both himself and the dog.

He opened his fingers and felt the rope slip out of his hand.

The disappointed groans of the helpers on shore followed him downriver. George sat on the shed roof, holding Wags, and wondered if he had just traded his own life for a chance to save the dog's.

But he could not abandon Wags. What would he tell Tilda when he saw her? *If* he ever saw her again.

Crash! The shed jerked violently as it hit the broken remains of a barn. George struggled to keep from falling off.

Smash! This time the shed was struck from the back by a telegraph pole. Wedged between the pole and the parts of the barn, the shed collapsed. Splintered pieces of the walls fell in all directions while the two sides of the roof clapped together to become one flat piece.

George, carrying Wags, jumped off the roof as it began to sink. He landed at the edge of a pile of broken buildings, furniture, and trees. The pile was floating on the water but did not seem to be moving forward any longer.

George began climbing across the wreckage, trying to reach the top of the heap. He lost his footing several times as the debris shifted. More rubble kept knocking into the back side, increasing the size of the pile and causing everything in it to change position on the water.

Each time George fell, he tried again. He found he could make better progress by crawling than by trying to walk. He couldn't carry Wags that way, but when he kept one arm around the dog, Wags crawled forward with him, scraping along on his belly.

Cries for help came from deep within the pile. George paused. He looked down, trying to see through the mass of rubbish. He could not see the people who called. He knew there was no way he could dig them out by himself.

"I can't reach you," George shouted to the unseen persons, "but I'm going for help. I'll send a rescue crew back for you." He hoped he would be able to remember where the voices came from.

The rubble was wet, and more water kept washing over George and Wags. Angry red scratches lined George's arms. Splinters from the wood pricked his palms. Twice Wags yelped with sudden pain as a sharp piece of wood or broken glass tore through his fur.

The sky darkened. I have to get to land before it's dark, George thought. It was hard enough to make progress when he could see. Each time he thought he had almost reached the top of the heap, more material hit the heap from behind and the whole pile shifted again, knocking him off balance.

Once he looked back and saw a boxcar smash into the rest of the rubble, causing the entire mass to quiver as if there had been an earthquake.

Seeing the boxcar brought fresh worries about Tilda. Where was the Day Express? Would he ever see his sister again?

CHAPTER

9

Warren and Betsy rushed away from the Keeton house. They ran to the end of the street and up the hill until they could see the river as it flowed into Johnstown.

A thick mist rose above the river now, blending with the rain until it was difficult to tell where the land ended and the sky began.

The dark mist rolled toward Johnstown, and they realized the mist preceded the cresting river.

"Look!" Warren shouted. "Here it comes!"

As the mist got closer, they could see

81

through it. Directly behind the mist, a huge tangle of broken buildings, trees, dead cattle, and other debris pushed toward Johnstown, all of it propelled by the churning river water.

Awestruck, Warren and Betsy watched for a moment as the torrent of water and smashed buildings approached. It plowed across the streets of Johnstown, demolishing everything in its path.

Wooden structures snapped into pieces. Telegraph poles toppled. Some of the smaller buildings were pushed off their foundations and floated away intact, many with people clinging to the roofs.

The air reverberated with the noise of wood splintering, metal grating on metal, human screams, and the terrible sound of water rushing forward.

The pile of debris smashed into the stone railroad bridge and stopped, causing the water behind it to back up even higher into Johnstown.

A man ran by pulling a pair of horses on a lead. "Run for your lives!" he called. "The dam has broken!"

His shout snapped Betsy and Warren out

of their shock and into action. "Take this," Betsy said, tossing the life ring to the man.

"Let's get out of here," Warren said. He reached for the On button of the Instant Commuter.

"We have to try to save Anna. We should have about five minutes before the water gets up here."

Pursued by the rapidly rising water, they dashed back to the Keeton home. Betsy's cap blew off, but she didn't bother to retrieve it. They pounded on the door.

This time Mrs. Keeton opened the door. Water covered the threshold and crept across the wooden floor. When Mrs. Keeton saw who it was, she started to shut the door.

Betsy cried out, "The dam has burst! You have three minutes to save your child!"

Mrs. Keeton's hand dropped from the door. "Anna!" she shouted. "Get to the garret."

Through the open door, Betsy and Warren saw Anna climb a wooden ladder. Her mother followed at her heels.

"We could give them our life jackets," Warren said. "We have the Instant Commuter. We can return home where it's safe and dry, but Anna and her mother have no way to escape."

"Let's do it," Betsy said as she pushed the door the rest of the way open.

The water swirled around them—first up to their ankles, then up to their knees— as they entered the Keetons' home. They mounted the ladder to the attic, with the water pursuing them.

The only light in the small upper room was what filtered in through a single window. Mrs. Keeton and Anna clutched the window ledge, with their faces pressed to the glass, staring out.

Mrs. Keeton turned to Betsy and Warren.

"Put these on," Betsy said, unbuckling the white straps that held the orange life jacket in place. Warren was undoing his life jacket, too.

"Who are you?" Mrs. Keeton asked. "Why are you here?"

"These will keep you and Anna from drowning," Warren explained. "They float on the water."

Betsy held her life jacket toward Anna.

"Put your arms through the holes," instructed.

The little girl looked questioningly at her mother.

"Do as they tell you," Mrs. Keeton said.

Anna stuck her arms through the holes and let Betsy buckle the strap. The adult-size life jacket was too large for the child. It reached nearly to her knees.

Water came through the attic door, covering the floor in seconds.

Warren handed his life jacket to Mrs. Keeton.

"Where did you get these?" she asked. "Why do you give them to us?"

"There's no time to explain," Betsy said. "We don't need them; we have another way to escape from the flood."

"Mama, look!" Anna said, her face against the window again. "Mrs. Williams and Bessie just went past. They're riding on the roof of their house."

"God have mercy," said Mrs. Keeton. She put her arms through the holes in Warren's life jacket.

The water flowed over the top of Warren's and Betsy's boots.

A loud crash came from directly beneath their feet. The attic room swayed slowly to one side and then back again.

"What was that?" Anna said.

"Something hit our house," her mother replied. "Hang on to me, Anna. We mustn't be separated." She reached for her daughter, without yet buckling the straps of her life jacket.

The water was nearly to their waists. "We have to leave," Warren said, "before the Instant Commuter gets wet."

"We never took any pictures of the flood," Betsy said.

"There's no time," Warren said.

Betsy knew Warren was right. She clasped her arms around Warren while he started the Instant Commuter. It began to hum.

The water rose faster, and the noise outside grew louder.

Warren fumbled in the plastic bag for the picture of Betsy's yard. Then he grabbed the probe.

Glass shattered. Betsy saw that an uprooted tree had crashed against the attic window, breaking it. Water gushed in.

The Flood Disaster

"Mama!" screamed Anna. "My hand is cut!"

"Hold on to me," Mrs. Keeton said. "We're going to jump."

"Good luck!" Betsy shouted.

"I'm bleeding!" Anna cried.

Mrs. Keeton grabbed Anna and, holding the child tightly, leaped out the window into the swollen river.

As they plunged forward toward the churning mass of water and debris, Anna's life jacket caught on a nail that jutted from the side of the window. The nail held Anna back as her mother tumbled forward. Anna was torn from her mother's arms.

Mrs. Keeton screamed, "Anna! Stay with me!" She strained toward her daughter, grabbed Anna's foot, and tried to pull Anna toward her.

The surging water pushed Anna back into the attic again. Her shoe came off in her mother's hand.

Betsy fumbled with Anna's life jacket, trying to free it from the nail.

"Hang on to me!" Warren said as he touched the probe to the picture.

Betsy turned away from Anna and held

on to Warren. She felt the familiar wind blow, and knew the Instant Commuter was working.

Usually Betsy closed her eyes against the wind. This time she did not. Through the broken window she saw Mrs. Keeton land feetfirst in the river, her arms still stretched upward trying to reach Anna. As Mrs. Keeton plummeted downward below the surface, her arms slipped out of the life jacket. It bobbed away, a bright bit of color in the dark river.

"Mama!" Anna screamed. "Help me!"

A wave rolled across her head, and she closed her eyes against the dirty water. She flailed her arms, desperately trying to find her mother. Her hand touched a piece of material under the water, and, thinking it was her mother's skirt, she grabbed it and held on with all her strength.

The swollen river poured over her head again, choking her, and filling her ears. Anna held fast. She heard her mother's voice shout, "Anna! Anna!" but the voice seemed to come from a great distance. How could Mama be far away when Anna was clinging to her skirt?

The Flood Disaster

She opened her mouth, gulping for air, and instead got a mouth full of water. She choked, unable to catch her breath.

She tried to hear Mama, but her mother's voice had disappeared, covered by the relentless pounding of the river and the sounds of buildings smashing. Was it her house she heard?

Anna felt as if she were floating, swirling in circles on top of the angry river. Gasping for breath, she opened her eyes just as two buildings smashed together, sending another wave of water over Anna's head.

Anna quit floating. She felt herself drift upward. The noise stopped and the river disappeared and she knew that she was headed for a new place, a strange place of peace, and quiet, and light.

Anna was tempted to let go and rise to that lovely place of peace. But she did not do it.

Her fingers still gripped the material that she thought was her mother's skirt.

Anna did not want to leave her mother.

CHAPTER

10

I am lucky to be alive, Tilda thought. If I had remained on the train another ten minutes, I would never have escaped.

Trembling with fear and relief, she stood on the hillside above East Conemaugh and looked at the havoc below.

Locomotives dipped and twirled like twigs in the water. A baggage car, tilted on its side, floated off downstream. Tilda knew her wicker trunk, containing all her clothes and personal belongings, was gone forever.

What should I do now? Tilda wondered.

The Flood Disaster

Where can I go? Where will I find food, and shelter?

Continuing on to her original destination was not possible. Not today, and maybe not ever. It would probably take weeks to rebuild the railroad tracks, and even when that was done, she didn't know if Mr. Robart would have need of her service.

Her employer's home may have washed away, too. Although it was above the dam, the lake would have backed up a long way before it was deep enough to burst the dam.

She hoped the three little boys were safe. Even though she had never met them, she had thought of them often in the last weeks and felt as if she knew them well.

Disappointment sent tears to her eyes as she realized that her dream of independence had washed away with the flood. She would not be spending the summer as a nursemaid. She would not be earning her own money. She would not be living away from home, and meeting new people.

I'll never have enough to fix the kitchen roof now, Tilda thought glumly, and then realized the foolishness of her complaint.

91

She needn't worry about the leaking roof; very likely, there would soon be no roof left to repair.

The rain pounded on Tilda's shoulders. She had never been so wet, or scared. She had never felt so alone.

How long would it take for the river and the mass of broken buildings that now floated on the river to reach Johnstown? Tilda felt a million miles from home, but she knew that the actual train ride had taken only about ten minutes. The rest of her day had been spent waiting on the tracks in East Conemaugh.

If it took ten minutes on the train, it should not be an impossible distance on foot. Perhaps she could walk to Johnstown.

When Tilda was first offered the nursemaid position, George had gone to the Adams Street schoolhouse and asked to borrow a map of the area. He brought it home, and they had studied it that night, pointing out the towns the train would pass through en route to her summer post.

Remembering that map, Tilda knew if she followed the river, she would come first to the small town of Woodvale and then to

The Flood Disaster

Prospect Hill, which overlooked Johnstown on the north. Of course, she needed to stay as high as possible, but she would try to keep the river in sight. Even when it was not visible through the trees, she still heard it.

If she stayed in the hills, walking only on high ground, there should be no danger. She would walk to Johnstown and search for George, and they would survive this calamity together.

Having a goal put fresh energy in Tilda's weary body, and, filled with determination, she began to hike toward Johnstown.

Walking was difficult with no path to follow, but it was better than standing still. At least the exercise kept her warm. Shrubs snagged her skirt, tearing it twice. She wished she could wear trousers, as George did. They were much more efficient in the outdoors than her long petticoat and dress. Tilda reached down and brought the back hem of her dress up between her legs and held it next to her waist.

How unladylike, she thought, and was glad neither her former teacher nor her pastor could see her. It did make the walking easier, and Tilda gathered her dress even higher and held it tightly against her chest.

Tilda knew from the map that East Conemaugh and Woodvale were on the north side of the river, while Johnstown was on the south. She decided to walk until she reached the stone railroad bridge at Johnstown. She would cross the river at that point.

And if the water was too high? If it had washed the bridge out?

No. Tilda pushed the thought out of her head. I won't think of that. I'll only think of finding George, and my little Wags. All I want in this world is to know that they are safe.

She plodded onward long after it grew dark, listening for the sound of the angry water to guide her.

She reached a cluster of people huddled around a fire and joined them, gratefully warming her hands. "Where am I?" she asked.

"Woodvale," a man replied, "or what's left of it."

"The flood destroyed the whole town," another man said. "Our homes are gone;

everything we worked for all our lives is gone. We have nothing but the clothes on our backs, and lucky to have those."

"It took less than five minutes," a woman said, through her tears. "Five minutes to crush an entire city. The only building not completely destroyed is the woolen mill, and it's half gone."

At last their woeful tales dwindled away, and someone thought to ask Tilda where she had come from.

"I walked from East Conemaugh," she said. "I was a passenger on the Day Express, but the tracks washed out and the train could go no farther. I'm walking back to Johnstown, to my home."

"You won't find it standing," someone predicted. "That river was gathering force as it went. The buildings it smashed here in Woodvale were carried along in the water to add force as it entered Johnstown. Once it was joined by Stony Creek, I cannot imagine the damage it would do."

"My brother is there," Tilda said. "He's all the family I have, and I must get to him."

"Won't you wait with us until daybreak?" a woman asked. "We can't offer you food, but you're welcome to share our fire."

"You're very kind," Tilda said, "but I'm going to walk on. George may need me."

Firelight made shadows dance on the sympathetic faces circling the blaze. Heads nodded. "If you must walk on," one man said, "stay high above the river. It may rise more before the night is over."

Warmed by the fire and their concern for her, Tilda resumed her journey. The night seemed blacker now. She turned her face to the heavens and saw only darkness through the rain. Even the moon and stars could not bear to look down on the destruction.

Branches snapped underfoot. As she walked, she made a game of pretending she was walking through her house. She went room by room, remembering every window and table. If it's all gone, Tilda thought, I still have my memories. Nothing can take those away.

She pictured her bed, with the hand-stitched quilt that Mummy had made for her. The quilt pattern, Log Cabin, was Tilda's favorite. She wished she could crawl beneath the bright colors, close her eyes, and feel snug and safe as she always had when Mummy came to say goodnight.

With her mind concentrating on home, Tilda forgot to listen for the rushing river. While she thought of the oak rocking chair and the metal bread pans and the thick braided rug, the noise of the river gradually grew dimmer, until it disappeared beyond the trees.

She tripped on a large root and fell forward into a soggy mess of mud. She tried to break her fall by extending her hands. Her left wrist twisted awkwardly as she landed on a heap of small branches that had blown down.

Tilda lay on the ground for a minute, rubbing her throbbing wrist. She knew she was fortunate not to have broken a bone. She wondered if she should continue on in the dark or go back to Woodvale and stay by the warm fire until daylight.

She could not judge how far she had walked. Was she more than halfway? Would it take longer to try to retrace her steps than to complete her journey?

Suddenly Tilda remembered reports of black bears in these hills, and wildcats.

I'll go on, she decided. I've come this far. Johnstown can't be too much farther.

She pushed herself upright and stood shivering, listening for the river. Ribbons of apprehension fluttered down Tilda's arms and legs. She could no longer hear the rush of water.

How is that possible? Tilda wondered. Did I go straight when the river curved? Am I disoriented, going in the wrong direction?

Panic pounded in Tilda's chest. Her plan of following the river had failed, and with no visible stars, she could not use the sky as her compass.

I'm lost, Tilda thought. I'm somewhere in the hills between Woodvale and Johnstown, but where? Which direction should I go?

CHAPTER

11

Betsy opened her eyes, relieved to see that she and Warren had landed, as planned, in Betsy's backyard. The Instant Commuter quit humming.

Even though she was safe again, Betsy shuddered at the horror she and Warren had witnessed. She had known from the books she had read that the Johnstown flood was a terrible tragedy. And she had known that Anna did not survive. But it was dreadful to be there and see it happen.

She had not expected to be so shaken. She often saw television news broadcasts about people killed in natural disasters. But they were unknown names.

Anna was no longer a name from distant history. She was a real little girl.

Betsy took a deep breath, trying to put the terrible scenes out of her mind.

Empress ran across the grass to greet Betsy but stopped about five feet away. The little dog growled.

"What's the matter with Empress?" Warren asked as he took off the backpack and put it on Betsy's picnic table.

"We must have scared her, appearing out of nowhere like this," Betsy said. She stepped away from Warren, and started toward the dog, but her right leg didn't move properly. It felt as if a weight were tied to her leg, holding it in place. She flexed her knees twice, to get the circulation moving.

Empress growled again.

"It's me, Empress," Betsy said. "Good dog." She held her hand toward Empress, so the dog could sniff it. Instead, Empress barked at Betsy and backed away from her.

Warren turned to look at Betsy. His mouth dropped open. He stared at her leg.

"What's the matter?" Betsy asked.

The Flood Disaster

Warren pointed at Betsy's leg. "That's why she's barking," he said.

Betsy looked down. An icy chill climbed her backbone.

A shadowy child stood beside her. The image of the child faded in and out, as if she were there and yet not there. The child's hand gripped the leg of Betsy's jeans.

Betsy watched as the image wavered into view. The child wore a white pinafore, but even as Betsy looked at the pinafore, she could also see the grass beneath the child. She saw the child, and saw through her at the same time.

"She has no face," Warren whispered.

"It's Anna," Betsy said. "She came home with us."

"It can't be Anna. Anna drowned."

Shocked by her own words, but knowing they were true, Betsy said, "It's Anna's ghost."

As they stared, the little girl faded again until all that was visible was the outline of the white pinafore and the small hand that still clutched Betsy's pant leg.

Betsy reached down and put her hand over the child's fingers, intending to pull the hand away from her pant leg. She drew her hand back in alarm.

"It's like touching an ice cube," she said.

She kicked her leg, trying to shake the hand free.

It hung on.

"Get her off me!"

When Empress heard the terror in Betsy's voice, she went into a frenzy of barking. She circled Betsy, staying about six feet away.

Warren grabbed the small hand. Even though he had been warned, he jumped when he felt how cold it was. Forcing himself to keep his hand on Anna's, he tried to pry the fingers loose from Betsy's jeans.

"I can't budge her," Warren said. "Her hand is locked in position as if the fingers were made of steel."

"What are we going to do?" Betsy felt like crying. Her leg grew cold near the area where Anna's hand was.

The ghost-child slowly reappeared. This time they saw her feet. She wore a high black laced shoe on one foot; the other foot had on only a stocking. They saw the dark green sleeve of her dress leading up to the pinafore.

"Anna," Betsy said, her voice quavering. "Anna, can you hear me?"

The little girl's face grew more visible. Her lips moved, but Betsy could not hear what she said.

"Empress, no bark," Betsy said.

Warren leaned forward with his head close to the child's. "What did you say?" he asked. "Say it again."

Betsy still heard nothing. Anna's face faded from view again. Her clothing shimmered briefly before it, too, disappeared. All that remained was the hand.

Betsy could see the child's fist, gripping Betsy's pant leg—but she could also see the tan denim, right through the hand.

Warren straightened, his face pale.

"Could you hear her?" Betsy asked.

Warren nodded. "She said, *Mama. Mama, help me.*"

Empress whined softly as Betsy and Warren stared at each other.

"She's drifting back and forth between this world and the next, isn't she?" Betsy said.

"I think so."

"She isn't alive, but she isn't really dead, either."

The area of cold on Betsy's leg grew larger. It felt the way her ankle had felt after she sprained it playing tennis and had to keep an ice pack on it for an hour. She shivered.

"We probably need to return to Johnstown at the same time we left," Warren said. "We'll stay just long enough to get Anna to let go."

"What if she doesn't?" Betsy whispered the words. "What if she stays with us? What if she comes home with us again?"

Warren didn't answer. How could he? The only answer he could think of was *If she doesn't let go, you'll have a ghost haunting you for the rest of your life.*

He did not want to say that to Betsy.

"We don't have a drawing or photo of Anna's house," Betsy said. "We can't go to the place we left, or the exact time."

Warren looked at his friend and saw his own panic reflected in her eyes. *Think,* Warren, he told himself. There's always more than one solution to a problem.

"Maybe we could bribe her to let go," Warren said.

"You mean, offer her money?" Betsy said. "Money isn't much use to a ghost."

"Not money. The doll. The one that Doc Keeton thinks is what his sister wanted."

"It's worth a try," Betsy agreed. "You'll have to go by yourself and convince Doc Keeton to part with it. I'm not leaving this yard. Not with her hanging on me."

"I'm on my way." He paused at the gate. "Are you sure you'll be all right here by yourself?" he asked.

"I'm not by myself," Betsy said. "That's the problem." She looked down at the small figure beside her, now visible again. The girl seemed made of glass.

"I'll ride my bike," Warren said. "It should only take me about ten minutes each way."

"Ten minutes to get there," Betsy said, "ten minutes home, and ten minutes to talk to Doc Keeton."

"Right. I'll be back in half an hour."

Half an hour. When Betsy was reading a good book, or hitting tennis balls against the garage wall, or playing with one of her foster dogs, half an hour was nothing. But half an hour with a ghost hanging on her leg sounded like half a lifetime. "Hurry," she said.

Warren let himself out the gate, dashed down the street to Gram's house, opened the garage, and mounted his bike. Pedaling as hard as he could, he headed toward Doc Keeton's house. I should have called him, he thought as he rode. What if he isn't home?

By the time Warren arrived, his shirt stuck to his back. He rang the doorbell, trying to compose himself.

"Warren!" Doc Keeton seemed pleased to see him. "Come in. Where's Betsy?"

Warren stepped inside. "I came to ask a huge favor," Warren said. "Betsy and I found a little girl who is perfect for that old-fashioned doll you have, the one you said is what your little sister always wanted."

His words flowed faster and faster, like the water spilling into Johnstown. "I know it's asking a lot, to expect you to give up a valuable doll that means so much to you,

106

and believe me, I wouldn't ask if it wasn't important." Warren paused for breath.

Doc Keeton's eyebrows raised in surprise. He stared at Warren.

I'm babbling, Warren thought. How can I expect him to believe me when I can't talk coherently? He forced himself to slow down.

"I can't tell you who the little girl is, but I *can* tell you that it's a matter of life or death, and I need to take the doll right now. Please."

Doc Keeton still said nothing. He walked to the shelf and removed the box containing the cherished doll. He opened the lid, folded back the tissue paper, and gazed at the doll. With tears in his eyes, he replaced the lid and handed the box to Warren.

"I trust you," he said.

"Thank you," Warren said. "I promise you that it's going to a child who wants it desperately. We chose her because she reminds us so much of what you said about Anna."

"Then you've made a good choice."

"I can't stay," Warren said. "I'll have to

come back later and tell you what happened."

Doc Keeton followed Warren to the door and watched as he rode away with the doll in his bike basket.

Not many people would have done what Doc Keeton just did, Warren thought as he rode. Lots of adults think kids can't be trusted, or they think anyone under twenty-one has no sense. Doc believed me, even without any explanation.

As he approached Betsy's house, Warren became more and more anxious. We started out to try to save Anna's life, Warren thought, and to help Doc Keeton by getting a picture of his sister. Instead, we've deprived Doc of his favorite doll, and possibly trapped Anna in some sort of in-between world where she has neither life nor peace. And if Anna didn't let go, Betsy would be stuck with a permanent ghost hanging on her leg. What a mess!

No matter how well he and Betsy tried to plan the Instant Commuter trips so they didn't end up in trouble, something unforeseen always happened.

If Betsy was forever haunted by the ghost,

The Flood Disaster

Warren knew he would be haunted by the knowledge that his actions were partly responsible. The Instant Commuter belonged to him. He should have refused to use it to go to Johnstown.

I won't use it again, Warren vowed. Never. It's the most incredible invention of the century, but there's too much that can go wrong.

He braked to a stop next to Betsy's back gate. He hoped the ghost was visible right now. He would show her the doll and tell her she could have it as soon as she let go of Betsy.

And what then? What if she let go but stayed nearby?

One thing at a time, Warren told himself. First we have to get her detached from Betsy's jeans.

CHAPTER

12

George's shirt caught on a twisted piece of barbed wire. Before he could disentangle himself, the pile moved again, and the wire shredded his sleeve, leaving a deep slash on his arm.

The roof of a factory slammed into the heap near him.

George saw dozens of other people, crawling like flies at a picnic, all caught in the massive pile. He also saw three dead bodies float past in the water.

After what seemed like an hour of struggle, George made it to the top of the heap. Even in the dim light he could see where he was. The rubble was accumulating against the stone bridge, unable to float on down the river. More rubble kept coming, adding to the pile that rose high above the water and stretched as far back as George could see, clear to the curve of the hill.

Now he knew which direction he had to go. If he could crawl across the top of the rubble until he reached the bridge, he could climb onto the bridge and from there to shore. As long as the bridge didn't wash out, he thought he would be safe.

"Stay with me, Wags," he said. "Good dog. We're going to make it, boy."

But knowing which way to crawl did not make the crawling any faster or easier. Not with the pile under his feet constantly shifting. Every few feet a gaping hole suddenly opened up, swallowing whatever was above it. Structures below the surface periodically collapsed, bringing down everything that rested on top of them.

George's ears pounded from the constant noise: buildings breaking, the terrified mooing of cattle, and—worst of all—people crying, and screaming, and begging for help.

Many people were trying to do exactly

what George was trying to do—crawl toward the bridge, and safety. Others, less fortunate, were trapped in the middle of the pile, with no way to get out.

"My house is gone," a woman sobbed. "My house is gone."

"Charlie!" a man called. "Charlie, can you hear me? Are you here?"

No one answered him.

A woman washed onto the pile near George. The woman, who was half-hysterical, clutched a child's shoe to her chest and kept saying, "Anna, Anna, my darling girl."

"Climb this way," George called to the woman. "You may be able to get onto the bridge."

She looked at George as if she were surprised to find another living person. George pointed in the direction of the bridge. "Try to go this way," he repeated. "We have to get to land before this rubble sinks or gets washed over the bridge."

The woman seized a table leg that protruded from the pile, and pulled herself out of the water.

"Don't try to stand," George said. "It's

easier to keep your balance if you stay on your hands and knees."

The words were barely out of his mouth when another building collided with the heap, knocking the woman back into the water. George watched her go under, thinking she had met her end. Seconds later her head bobbed to the surface again. George snatched a piece of lumber and extended it into the water toward the woman.

"Swim this way!" he shouted. "Maybe I can pull you out." The woman had trouble maneuvering in the water, but she managed to swim close enough to grasp the other end of the board.

George pulled her toward him. She grabbed the side of an iron bed that was stuck in the pile, and pulled herself onto the heap again. He was amazed to see that she still clutched the child's shoe in her hand.

Would they ever get to shore? Each time George made progress toward the bridge, more debris smashed into the pile, making it higher and wider. For every yard George moved forward, he stumbled at least that far backward. He tried to climb up but kept sliding down as he was knocked off balance.

A wall of water cascaded over him from behind. He clutched Wags, braced himself, and clung to a tree trunk that stuck partway out of the pile. He expected to be swept back into the river, but the wave crashed over him and then, its forward movement stopped by the heap of debris, crashed back again.

When the water subsided, he heard a great commotion above him on the bridge. The woman with the child's shoe had been washed forward far enough to be reached by the rescuers who lined the bridge. They cheered as they pulled her onto the bridge.

What good fortune for her, George thought, and wished he and Wags might be washed upward, too.

It did not happen.

Night fell. Wags refused to go on. He simply lay where he was, put his muzzle down on his paws, and closed his eyes.

He's exhausted, George realized. And so am I. We aren't going to make it to the bridge. It takes too much energy to keep climbing up, only to get knocked down again.

All I can hope to do is keep from drowning. If I can hang on to the pile, and to Wags, and keep our heads above water through the night, surely we'll be rescued in the morning. By then the water will start to subside, or people will come in boats to rescue us.

The tree trunk that he had held on to during the last big wave seemed a good place to stay. He straddled it, with Wags in front of him.

All the exertion had made him terribly thirsty.

"All this water," he said to Wags, "and we have none to drink."

It *did* feel good to sit still. He hadn't realized how much his muscles ached. When the pile shifted, he leaned over Wags and held on to the tree. He imagined this was what it would be like to ride a bucking horse.

The shouts for help continued all around him. They sounded more frightening in the dark. George longed to put his hands over his ears and blot out everything around him, but he didn't dare let go of Wags, or of the tree.

Wags lifted his head, sniffing the air. He whined and pawed at George's arm.

"I know you're hungry, boy," George said. "So am I." He wished he had not left his dinner pail up on the hill. That shepherd's pie would taste mighty good right now.

The tree lurched. Water splashed across George's shoulders.

Wags barked. It was his short, sharp warning bark—the sound he made when a stranger came to the door.

George put a hand on the dog's head, trying to calm him.

Wags barked again.

George smelled smoke. How could there be fire in the midst of a flood? With water covering every building in town, what could possibly burn?

He inhaled again. It was definitely smoke. He turned his head from left to right, trying to see which direction the smoke came from.

He looked behind him, and gasped. Bright flames leaped skyward a few yards away.

The Flood Disaster

The pile of rubble had caught fire.

George could not fathom how a fire would have started in the middle of a flooded river. With so much water around it, and the rain still pounding down, he didn't think the fire could burn for long.

But it did burn, flaming higher and brighter, until he could tell that the entire mass of floating rubble would soon be a blazing hill of horror for anyone trapped on it.

Screams arose behind him, above him, and below him, filling the night air with agony. The pile was impassable now, consumed by flames.

George was faced with an impossible choice: try to climb through the flames and reach the bridge or jump into the flooded river.

If he had been unable to climb across the shifting mass before, how could he expect to do it now when the pile was burning? His clothing would surely catch fire long before he reached the bridge.

If he jumped into the river, he would probably drown.

The heat from the fire blistered George's

cheeks. Wind pushed the flames forward and back again. Wags threw his head back and yowled a long, mournful howl.

The fire seemed to have started near the center of the huge pile and was now spreading outward. George crawled away from it, toward the edge of the heap. Wags stayed beside him, without any urging.

The flames followed. George wondered if the fire was started by overturned coal stoves from the demolished houses that were part of the pile. Or perhaps the fire began with oil from a railroad tank car. Even with rain above and floodwater below, the fire fed on the thousands of pieces of dry, broken lumber from the smashed buildings.

George crawled as close to the edge of the pile of rubble as he could get. He gathered Wags into his arms and leaped forward into the swollen, black water.

CHAPTER

13

Exhausted, Tilda leaned against a tree trunk, hoping the tree would keep some of the rain off her. She closed her eyes and concentrated on sound.

How could she have walked too far away to hear the flooded river that had been so dreadfully loud before? Had the river turned, carrying its load of destruction beyond where she could hear it? Or had the flood simply outdistanced her, traveling faster than she could walk? Perhaps the high water, with its burden of wreckage, was far ahead of her now.

Maybe I am still going the right way,

Tilda thought. Maybe I can't hear the river anymore because the flood has passed.

She shivered. Whether she was going toward Johnstown or not, she needed to keep moving in order to stay warm. Gathering up her skirt again, she headed on.

A glimmer of light, far ahead and to her left, caught her attention. Tilda had no idea what it could be, but she walked toward it. As she continued, the light grew bigger and brighter, and she realized it was a fire.

At first she thought she was headed toward another group of survivors like the ones she had met at Woodvale—people who were gathered around a bonfire to keep warm. But as she got closer, the fire leaped higher and spread wider, and she knew it was much more than a mere bonfire.

Soon she heard sound again, coming from the same direction as the fire. It was not the sound of rushing water; it was buildings breaking up, and smashing together.

Tilda ran toward the bright light, certain that she was approaching Johnstown. The noise grew louder and more horrible as human screams mingled with the din of destruction.

The Flood Disaster

By the time Tilda realized where she was—on the side of Prospect Hill, with the railroad bridge below her in the distance—it was so light from the fire that she could clearly see her destination.

She stared down at the frightful scene. The broken buildings, the uprooted trees, and the wrecked railroad cars from East Conemaugh and Woodvale were now piled up against the massive stone arches of the bridge. The pile had become a dam, causing the floodwaters to back up across Johnstown. Worst of all, the pile was ablaze.

One glance toward the city told her that the Johnstown she had always known no longer existed. She sought out her favorite landmarks, and did not find them. The library was gone, and the fire station.

The Hulbert House, the grandest hotel in town, was gone. Earlier in the day the four-story brick hotel had seemed to be the safest place for the family from her church to wait out the storm. Tilda wondered what their fate had been.

Even the massive factories of the Cambria Iron Works had crumbled into the water.

The part of town where Tilda lived was too far back from the fire to be illuminated, but she knew that it could not have escaped.

Walking in a daze, she slowly descended the hill toward the bridge. The lower part of the hill was slippery with mud and littered with debris. The water must have slapped against the hillside and then descended.

She kept her eyes on the fire, unable to look away from the horror. She saw people trapped on the burning debris and realized they could either jump into the raging river, and likely drown, or they would burn to death. She watched, horrified, as people flung themselves into the water, sometimes with their clothing already afire.

I must help them, Tilda thought, and she ran pell-mell downhill, slipping and sliding in the muddy mess, until she arrived out of breath at the bridge.

She looked around for something—anything—that she could extend into the water so that a person could grasp it and hang on while she pulled him to shore.

The best she could find was a long piece

of lumber, apparently a beam from one of the broken structures. Dragging it behind her, she went as close to the edge of the water as she could.

Other would-be rescuers already lined the edge of the water, offering planks, long pipes, and branches to those floundering in the river. "Swim this way!" they yelled. "We'll pull you out!" Their shouts of encouragement helped blot out the screams of terror that rose from the fire.

Tilda saw a small boy clinging to a floating telegraph pole, and thrust her board toward him. The boy let go of the pole, kicking his feet and flailing his arms as he tried to reach Tilda's board. His head disappeared under the churning water, but popped up again seconds later.

Tilda stretched forward until she was in danger of falling in herself. Her arms ached from holding the heavy beam above the surface of the water.

The boy reached the board. His weight on the end of it nearly caused Tilda to drop her end.

She pulled with all her might. "I need help!" she cried.

A man standing nearby saw her problem. He let go of his own piece of wood and helped Tilda pull the boy ashore.

The child collapsed, sobbing, in Tilda's arms. All his clothing except a tattered pair of trousers had been torn from his body. Tilda removed her petticoat and wrapped it around the boy. Her petticoat was wet, torn, and dirty—but it was better than nothing.

Knowing she had no more strength to pull anyone else from the river, she led the boy uphill far enough to be safe. She sat on the ground with her back against a tree and held the child on her lap. He looked about four years old, but he could not stop crying to answer Tilda's questions.

Below her the shouts of the rescuers continued. "Hang on!"

"Here comes a dog. Use the net on the dog!"

"This way! Try to swim this way!"

"I'm losing my grip—help me pull this one in!"

Their voices mixed with the sounds from the burning pile until Tilda could no longer sort one from the other. She gave up trying and concentrated her energies on soothing the child in her lap.

"Hush now," she said, stroking his wet hair. "You're safe here with me." She hummed the lullaby that her mother had always sung to her at bedtime. Gradually the boy's sobs subsided.

I am needed as a nursemaid, after all, Tilda thought.

Betsy watched over the fence for Warren to return. She opened the gate as he got off his bike.

"Thank goodness you're back," Betsy said.

Empress ran to greet Warren, carefully keeping her distance from Betsy.

Warren looked first at Betsy's right leg. The small hand still clung to her jeans, but the rest of the child was invisible.

"She came into view once while you were gone," Betsy said, "but she was fainter than before. Then she faded away again, all except her hand. My leg is freezing."

"I got the doll," Warren said. "As soon as Anna appears again, we'll tell her she can have the doll if she lets go of you."

"I changed my mind," Betsy said. "We can't give her the doll. Not here."

"I broke the world's record for bicycle speed," Warren said as he wiped the sweat from his neck, "and now you tell me you've changed your mind."

"If we offer the doll to Anna's ghost and she lets go of me in order to get it, she'll still be here, with us. Even if she isn't hanging on to my jeans, I don't want her here."

"I don't want her here, either."

"While you were gone I figured out a better plan. We have to go back to Johnstown."

"No way. I am never—"

Betsy interrupted. "It's the only way to get rid of Anna's ghost. We'll touch the probe to the same drawing of Johnstown that we used before. We'll arrive at the same place and the same time as we did then: near the church *before* the flood began. And Anna will be alive and home with her mother."

Warren wondered why he hadn't thought of that plan himself. Even though he had vowed, only minutes earlier, never to use the Instant Commuter again, he knew

The Flood Disaster

Betsy was right. It was the only sure way to free themselves from the ghost.

"As soon as she's off my leg, we'll use the Instant Commuter to come home. Without the ghost."

"Betsy," he said, "you are a genius."

"In Roman mythology," Betsy said, "a genius was a spirit. Every baby born was assigned a genius to protect him and guide him to happiness. The genius acted as a middleman between the person and the gods."

"You can be my genius," Warren said, "and protect me in Johnstown."

"I almost went without you," Betsy said. "Once I realized how easy it would be to get rid of the ghost, I didn't want to wait for you to get back."

"I'm glad you waited. We need to stay together, in case something goes wrong."

"Something *always* goes wrong on these trips," Betsy said.

"Not this time. This time it will be zip there, unload the ghost, and zip home."

"I wish we didn't have to go at all."

"This will be our last trip through time

and space," Warren promised as he put the backpack on. "It's too dangerous."

"I agree."

While Warren started the Instant Commuter, Betsy put the doll in the plastic bag with her camera. Why not give the doll to Anna, as Doc Keeton had always wished he could do? She held the bag tightly as the Instant Commuter began to hum.

Warren touched the probe to the area behind St. John's Church on the old drawing. A minute later he and Betsy stood once more in Johnstown, on May 31, 1889.

"She's gone!" Betsy said as she ran her hand down her pant leg. "Our plan worked."

Warren reached in his pocket for the picture of Betsy's yard. "Let's get out of here."

"Wait," Betsy said. "We know we have about ten minutes before the flood hits. And we know where Anna is. I want to give her the doll."

"Are you crazy? We need to get home, while we can."

"Anna is going to die today, in the flood," Betsy said. "We have the doll she's always wanted. Instead of giving Doc Keeton the picture of Anna by herself, maybe we can give him one of Anna with the doll."

Warren thought about Doc Keeton, and how Doc's father had always wished he could give his daughter the doll she wanted. He remembered how Doc had trusted him, without question. "I promised Doc I was going to give the doll to a little girl who wants it desperately," he said.

"Then let's do it. Leave the Instant Commuter on, so we can go quickly, if we need to."

Warren and Betsy ran along the same streets they had run on earlier. This time they knew exactly where to go.

They pounded on the Keetons' door. When Anna opened it, Betsy said, "Hello, Anna. This is for you."

She handed the doll to the astonished child.

"It's a present," Warren said. "From your brother."

"I don't have a brother," Anna said, but she cradled the doll in her arms, her face glowing with happiness.

Betsy snapped a picture.

"Who is it, Anna?" called Mrs. Keeton.

"Show the doll to your mother," Betsy said.

When Anna turned away, Warren put the Instant Commuter probe on the picture of Betsy's backyard.

As they began their journey back to the present, Betsy heard Anna's excited voice telling her mother about the doll. The voice grew fainter as Betsy and Warren moved through time and space, and then it disappeared.

CHAPTER

14

George surfaced, gasping for air. He saw Wags, dog-paddling with his snout pointed up, headed for shore. The dog moved downstream faster than he went toward land. I can't help him, George thought. I can only try to save myself.

A long section of wooden fence rode the water nearby, and George swam as hard as he could to reach it. Clinging to the fence, he was pulled along with the flow. He couldn't control where he went, but he could keep his head above the water.

His arms ached; his legs were numb from

the cold water. He hung on, certain that the fence was his only hope of survival. He tried to spot Wags but could not see him.

God of all creatures, George prayed, *please watch over little Wags and keep him safe.*

The prayer had barely left his lips when the fence collided with a floating house. Instantly another house smashed into the fence from behind, catching George between the two buildings.

Pain shot through his legs. He pulled himself up onto one of the houses, with his legs dragging uselessly behind. He knew they were broken. Both of them.

Dizzy from the pain, George lay down on the roof of the house and, with the rain pelting his back, lost consciousness.

He awoke that night, aware that the house he lay on was no longer moving. Had he washed ashore?

"Help!" he called.

No one answered. No one came. George passed out again.

The rain stopped, at last. As morning light arrived, Tilda still sat on the muddy hillside, with her arms wrapped around the sleeping boy.

The horrible noise of the night was gone, although the fire still blazed.

Her stomach rumbled from hunger, and she wondered if she would ever feel warm again. Across the river the remains of Johnstown were nearly unrecognizable.

Clouds of smoke from the burning heap floated upward.

Tilda saw that she was not alone on Prospect Hill. Other people stood or sat nearby, gazing at the unbelievable sight below.

The little boy stirred, and woke. Tilda saw the fear flash into his eyes as he remembered where he was, and why.

"What is your name?" she asked.

"Andrew."

"The worst is over, Andrew," Tilda said, hoping her words were true.

"Where are Mama and Papa?" he asked.

"I don't know. We'll try to find them."

A mournful yowl rose from the hill behind her. Turning, Tilda saw a dog with his nose tilted up, howling his despair. Soon he was joined by other homeless dogs who prowled the hillside, howling dismally.

133

Although the sound was full of anguish, it filled Tilda with hope. If these dogs had somehow escaped, then perhaps Wags was safe, and George, as well.

She wondered how the dogs came to be on the hill. Had they run to safety before the flood hit? Had they been plucked from the water by rescuers? She remembered hearing a man shout something about a dog the night before.

Tilda eased Andrew from her lap and stood up. Her stiff joints ached from the cold dampness. She knew she needed to move around, both to keep warm and to loosen up.

"I'm going to look for my brother and my dog," she told Andrew. "Would you like to help me?"

"What's your dog's name?"

"Wags. He's a small tan terrier, and he likes little boys."

"Will he like me?"

"I'm certain he will. We'll look for your parents, too."

"All right. I'll go with you. But I would like my breakfast first, if you please."

Breakfast. The very word made Tilda's

mouth water. She wondered how long it would be before she and Andrew had something—anything—to eat.

"There is no breakfast," she said. And no dinner, either, she thought glumly. Her mouth felt as dry as dust, but there was no water fit to drink. The flood had left total destruction in its wake.

Tilda and Andrew tramped the hillside searching for George and Wags and Andrew's family. Hundreds of other people did the same, looking for loved ones.

Below them the water gradually subsided, revealing the ruins of Johnstown. Only a few buildings stood where they had been the day before. Tilda recognized the Methodist Church, and the iron company's brick office.

Tilda plucked clothing for Andrew from one of the uprooted trees that lined the banks of the river. It fit poorly, but it was better than wearing only torn trousers and a petticoat.

Tilda tried to remain hopeful about finding George and Wags alive, but it was difficult not to be discouraged amid reports of hundreds of unidentified bodies being found all along the path of the flood.

Besides the burning pile of rubbish at the bridge, other fires had broken out in different places.

A terrible stench rose from the mud, making Tilda feel sick to her stomach.

Before long, people who lived high in the hills, whose homes had escaped, brought down food and water. Tilda gratefully accepted a cup of milk for Andrew, water for herself, and a piece of bread for both of them.

A group of men strung a rope bridge over the river and crawled across to rescue people stranded on rooftops that were still surrounded by water.

Tilda and Andrew spent the rest of the day searching for survivors.

On Sunday morning they attended an outdoor church service conducted by a preacher whose church was demolished. A single candle served as the altar. It was comforting to sing the familiar hymns and to pray for the safety of those who were missing.

Rumors of looting were rampant, but

The Flood Disaster

Tilda saw only people trying to help. When she wasn't looking for George, she let Andrew play in the mud while she assisted a group of women who were caring for the injured.

The Pennsylvania Railroad got a track open to Johnstown and relief trains arrived carrying supplies and people to help.

Governor Foraker sent hundreds of tents. Tilda and Andrew shared one with twelve other survivors. Although she felt fortunate to have shelter, her concern for George increased with each passing hour. Where was he? What had happened to him?

The next day Tilda and Andrew crossed the bridge to Johnstown. Silently they passed by a line of wooden coffins on the railroad station platform, searching for Andrew's parents, and for George. To Tilda's great relief, she did not recognize any of the dead, nor did Andrew.

As they left the station, Andrew suddenly shouted, "Uncle Edward!" He released Tilda's hand and raced toward a tall, bearded man.

"Andrew!" The man dropped to his knees and enfolded the boy in his arms.

Tears of joy streamed down the man's face. "Oh, Andrew, I thought you had drowned."

"Tilda saved me," Andrew said. "She pulled me from the river and found clothes for me and sang me to sleep." He grabbed Tilda's hand and pulled her closer. "This is Uncle Edward."

"I'm Tilda Minnigan. I am so glad you are reunited with your nephew."

"I thank you from the bottom of my heart," the man said, "for helping this child."

"Where's Mama, and Papa?" Andrew asked. "Where's Aunt Rachel?"

"They're gone," the man said, his voice breaking. "The whole family's gone, except for me and you."

Andrew started to cry. His uncle picked him up and, holding him close, walked away.

Tilda was glad Andrew had found his uncle, but the news of Andrew's family made her all the more anxious about George and Wags.

She clung to the hope that George was alive. Perhaps he was injured and unable to look for her. Perhaps he was being cared for in another town, just as the injured here were being helped, and when he was well enough to come home, he would.

Home. Tilda decided to try to find the spot where her home had been.

With the streets buried in mud and debris, and most of the buildings destroyed, it was not easy to find even so well-known a place as her own yard.

Household items littered the entire area. Toys, broken dishes, and pieces of machinery poked from the filth. A grand piano lay on its back, like a bug with its legs in the air.

Even worse were the animal carcasses. Tilda had a tender heart for animals, and it grieved her to see bodies of horses, cows, cats, dogs, pigs, and chickens lying in the muck. There were too many humans in need of burial; nobody could tend to the animals. Tilda walked along what she thought had been her street, looking for landmarks and finding none.

Nothing familiar remained. Her neighbors' homes were gone, as was her own. The trees had been uprooted and the houses crushed and carried away. Tilda had been born in that house; until this week she had slept there every night of her life.

When she reached what she thought had been her own yard, she poked about in the mud with a stick, hoping to unearth something familiar. She found a book, too muddy to read, and a half-full keg of nails. Neither had come from her household, and she wondered if she was in the wrong place or if her own belongings were being discovered farther downstream.

Overcome with despair, she sat on the nail keg and wept. For Andrew's sake, she had held back her emotions. Now they spilled out and her body shook with sobs as she buried her face in her hands.

Something cold and wet touched the side of her face. Startled, Tilda dropped her hands and looked.

"Wags!" she cried. "Wags, is it really you?"

The dog's fur was matted; dried clumps of mud clung to his paws. He held one front foot up, as if it were injured, and there was a large gash across one ear. But his tail wagged joyfully at the sound of Tilda's voice.

The Flood Disaster

Not caring that Wags was filthy, Tilda scooped him into her arms and held him close. "Oh, Wags," she said, "you found your way home, even though home isn't here any longer."

Wags licked the salty tears from Tilda's cheeks.

CHAPTER

15

George opened his eyes and saw that he was in a tent. He lay on a cot; splints kept his legs straight.

George moaned; a woman came to his side. She offered him a drink of water, which George sipped.

"Where am I?" George asked.

"You're in a hospital tent, in Sang Hollow."

"I must look for my sister," George said, "in Johnstown." He started to sit up, groaned, and lay back down.

"Lie as still as you can," the woman said.

The Flood Disaster

"Rescue crews are helping those who need it. Supplies have come from Pittsburgh, along with nurses and doctors from the American Red Cross. Temporary shelters are being built in Johnstown."

George took another sip of water, closed his eyes, and drifted back to sleep.

Tilda shared what little food she received with Wags. He stayed so close to her that if she stopped suddenly, he ran into her.

She viewed more bodies at the Adams Street schoolhouse, and wept when one was Mrs. Dopkins.

She spent her days, as did all able-bodied survivors, on the enormous job of cleaning up Johnstown.

Whenever she saw someone she knew, they greeted each other joyfully, even if they had not been close friends before the flood. Tilda always asked if they had seen George. The answer was always "No."

Three weeks after the flood, as she piled broken boards to be burned, Wags gave a strange high "yip" and ran off.

"Wags, come back," Tilda called.

Then she saw where Wags was going.

George, using crutches for support, walked slowly toward her.

Betsy and Warren packed all the Instant Commuter instructions and diagrams in a cardboard box. They put the Instant Commuter on top of them and taped the box shut.

"When Grandpa invented the Instant Commuter," Warren said, "he envisioned only the good that it could do. He never thought about the potential danger."

"I'm glad we aren't going to use it again," Betsy said, "but I'm a little sad, too. The Instant Commuter trips were the most amazing days of my life."

"Even with all the scary times," he said, "the Instant Commuter was quite an adventure."

"I wish we could have saved Anna's life."

"So do I. Maybe it isn't possible to go back in time and change history. Maybe we should never have tried."

Warren put the taped box on his closet shelf and closed the door.

He looked at Betsy, wondering what to do next.

"I'm thirsty," she said.

"Do you want a soda?"

"No, thanks. I'll have a glass of water." As she poured it, Betsy said, "Did you know that the average horse drinks between nine and fifteen gallons of water every day?"

Warren shook his head. "How," he said, "would I know that?"

"Read the encyclopedia, like I do."

Doc Keeton stared at the photograph. It was his doll; he was sure of that. Every detail matched perfectly.

He was equally sure that the picture had been taken long ago. The child's frilly pinafore, her hairstyle, and her high button shoes were clearly from the past. It wasn't only the child's clothing that convinced him; it was the old look of the house in the background. An oil lantern hung on a crude hook by the unpainted door.

Could this really be Anna, as it said on the back of the picture? If so, there was only one explanation: Warren and Betsy had somehow gone back in time, found Anna, and given her the doll.

Doc reached for the telephone, hesitated, then withdrew his hand. If Warren and Betsy wanted him to know what they had done, they would have brought the picture to him rather than mailing it with no return address.

Warren had acted upset the day he took the doll, and was clearly relieved when Doc did not ask him to explain.

I won't ask now, either, Doc decided. I'll accept this astonishing gift and treasure it, but I won't question how it came about.

He looked at the picture again, feeling a warm glow at the knowledge that little Anna, at long last, had received the doll she wanted.

To learn more about the Johnstown flood:

Historical Catastrophes: Floods
Walter R. Brown and Billye W. Cutchen
Addison-Wesley (Reading, MA, 1975)

The Story of the Johnstown Flood
R. Conrad Stein
Children's Press (Chicago, IL, 1984)

The Johnstown Flood
David McCullough
Simon & Schuster (New York, NY, 1987)

Johnstown: The Day the Dam Broke
Richard O'Connor
J. B. Lippincott Co. (Philadelphia, PA, 1957)

The Johnstown Flood Museum
P.O. Box 1889
Johnstown, PA 15907–0889
http://www.artcom.com/museums/nv/gl/
15901.htm

About the Author

PEG KEHRET's popular novels for young people are regularly nominated for state awards. She has received the Young Hoosier Award, the Golden Sower Award, the Iowa Children's Choice Award, the Sequoyah Award, the Pacific Northwest Young Readers' Choice Award, the Minnesota Maud Hart Lovelace Award, and the New Mexico Land of Enchantment Award. She lives with her husband, Carl, and their animal-friends in Washington state, where she is a volunteer at the Humane Society and the Society for the Prevention of Cruelty to Animals. Her two grown children and four grandchildren live in Washington, too.